YOU ARRESTED MY ATTENTION

A GOTHIC VAMPIRE ROMANCE

V. P. NIGHTSHADE

SOHMER PUBLISHING

Copyright

First published by Sohmer Publishing 2026

You Arrested My Attention
EPUB ISBN: 978-1-960139-31-3
Paperback ISBN: 978-1-960139-32-0
Audio ISBN: 978-1-960139-33-7
First edition

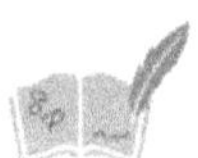

Contents

Epigraph

The Obsession of Attention

Some people mistake attention for something gentle.
A glance.
A passing curiosity.
A momentary warmth.
They are wrong.
Real attention alters things.
It learns the sound of your footsteps before you arrive.
It notices which window you stand beside when the rain begins.
It remembers the exact shape of silence after you leave a room.
I had forgotten distraction.
Forgotten the humiliating gravity of wanting to look twice.
Then you arrived carrying the ruins of previous life in your hands
and thanked the dead for giving you somewhere to sleep.
God.
Do you understand what devotion becomes
when it is born inside something immortal?
Not affection.
Not appetite.
Instead...
It bccomcs architccturc.
A cathedral of need built carefully around one living heartbeat.
And now the building listens for you.
The records wait for you.
The dark rearranges itself when you enter.
As do I.

— David Caesarius

Chapter I
Marceaux House

The rain started before Ember crossed into Louisiana and followed her all the way to New Orleans, like something patient.

By the time the taxi left her in front of Marceaux House, the city had dissolved into silver-black water and trembling gold reflections. Rain slid down the wrought-iron balconies in glittering streams. Ancient brick sweated damp beneath the gas lamps lining the narrow street. Across the avenue, marble crypts rose behind ornate cemetery gates like drowned monuments waiting beneath the storm.

Ember climbed out with two suitcases, a leather portfolio tube, and the sharp awareness that she owned exactly four hundred and twelve dollars.

The taxi disappeared immediately.

Of course it did.

She stood beneath the overhang of the building entrance and stared up at the faded brass letters mounted over the old arched doorway.

MARCEAUX HOUSE.

The inheritance had sounded fake when the lawyer called.

Your great-grandfather left you the apartment.

Not a huge amount of money.

No stocks to speak of.

An apartment.

Monthly allowance if you take up residence there.

Taxes for a decade paid upfront.

Not in New York City.

In New Orleans.

She had almost hung up on him.

Three weeks earlier, she'd still been in Brooklyn trying to salvage her life from a condemned building and a terminated gallery position.

Three weeks earlier, she'd spent nights scrolling apartment listings she couldn't afford while pretending panic wasn't chewing holes through the lining of her stomach and working its way through her ribs.

And now she stood in front of a gothic building across from a huge cemetery while thunder rolled over the city like distant artillery.

Life was strange enough to feel scripted sometimes.

The front doors groaned when she pushed inside.

The lobby smelled like rainwater, old wood, candle wax, and something darker beneath it all. Age, maybe. Like time soaked into wallpaper.

She hadn't blinked when the lawyer told her the apartment was on the fourth floor at the top of the building. After all, he had stated that the large apartment covered half of the building, sharing the floor with only one other apartment. She remembered his soft southern drawl, "Think of it like a penthouse there in New York. It's the best!"

Now she just stared in disbelief.

A cage elevator waited behind wrought-iron latticework, though the cardboard sign attached to it read OUT OF ORDER in elegant handwritten script.

Naturally.

Ember dragged her luggage toward the staircase.

The old hardwood stairs curved upward beneath amber wall sconces. Rain tapped softly against the stained-glass landing windows between floors. Somewhere above her, music drifted softly through the building.

Vinyl.

Not the clarity of digital sound.

Actual vinyl.

Low and melancholy.

A man's voice singing somewhere behind static and rain.

By the third floor, her lungs burned.

Halfway to the fourth, one of her suitcase wheels snapped off completely.

"Oh, come on."

The bag slammed sideways against the stair rail.

Ember closed her eyes.

Counted to three.

When she looked up again, someone stood at the top of the staircase on the landing of the fourth and final floor.

Still.

Watching her.

He wore black from throat to polished shoes. Dark wool coat. One hand resting lightly against the carved banister. The low amber lighting sharpened the severe angles of his face into something almost unreal.

Tall.

Lean.

Beautiful in the dangerous way old churches were beautiful.

Not safe to linger inside too long.

Rainwater darkened strands of black hair near his temple as though he'd stepped inside only moments ago. His eyes settled on her with unnerving steadiness.

Not startled.

Not curious.

Intent.

Ember became abruptly aware of how disheveled she looked.

Wet hair.

Smudged eyeliner.

One broken suitcase.

Anxiety wrapped in black wool.

The silence stretched.

Then his gaze dropped to the collapsed wheel beside her luggage.

"I think," he said quietly, "your suitcase surrendered."

His voice startled her more than his appearance had.

Low.

Cultured.

Light English accent.

Smooth enough to feel expensive.

Ember laughed before she meant to.

"Traitorous behavior, honestly."

The corner of his mouth shifted faintly.

Not a full smile.

Something smaller.

More dangerous.

He descended the stairs toward her without hurry.

Every movement measured.

Controlled.

When he reached for the broken suitcase, his fingers brushed hers briefly.

Cold.

Not winter cold.

Stone-shadow cold.

Her breath caught before she could stop it.

His eyes flicked upward immediately.

He noticed.

Of course, he noticed.

"Apartment 4B?" he asked.

"Yes."

"I'm across the hall."

He lifted the suitcase effortlessly.

Ember stared at him for half a second too long.

"That seems unfair."

A pause.

"What does?"

"You making that look easy while I nearly died four stairs ago."

Another almost-smile.

"You're dramatic."

"You haven't seen me at my full potential yet."

That finally earned something warmer from him. Not laughter exactly. But close enough to reshape his mouth into something devastating.

He resumed climbing.

Ember followed behind him, trying not to stare at the broad line of his shoulders beneath the dark coat.

Failing slightly.

The fourth-floor hallway looked preserved from another century. Dark floral wallpaper. Brass sconces. Thick runner carpets muffling footsteps. Rain moving softly beyond tall arched windows at the far end of the corridor.

Her door opened into the half of her apartment that shared the cemetery-facing side of the building.

Across from it: his door.

Black.

Unmarked.

Elegant.

He set her luggage down gently outside 4B.

"Thank you," Ember said, fishing through her coat pocket for the key. "Seriously."

"You're welcome."

She finally managed to unlock the apartment and pushed the door inward.

The place stole her breath immediately.

High ceilings.

Massive bay windows in the living area overlooking the cemetery.

Dark hardwood floors.

Built-in bookshelves.

Crown molding.

Moon-pale lightning flashed beyond the rain-streaked glass, illuminating marble crypts visible outside below.

"Oh my God," she whispered.

"This is the top floor of a refurbished antebellum. Our apartments are the only two on this floor. You had not seen photographs?" He asked.

Ember shook her head slowly. "The lawyer only sent legal documents."

His gaze moved across her face carefully.

Studying reactions.

"You like it."

It wasn't a question.

"I think," she said softly, "I might actually survive here."

Something shifted in his expression then.

Small.

Almost invisible.

But she felt it.

Like tension tightening beneath silk.

He leaned one shoulder lightly against her doorway.

"David Caesarius," he said.

Right.

Names.

She'd nearly forgotten normal human interaction requirements.

"Ember Grant."

His eyes held hers.

Longer than most people would.

"Ember," he repeated quietly.

As if testing the shape of it.

The rain deepened outside.

Somewhere below them, thunder rolled through the cemetery streets.

Then David glanced once toward the enormous bay windows inside her apartment.

"We have the best view in the building."

Ember looked past him toward the expanse of crypts glimmering beneath the storm. "It's the most beautiful thing I have seen in a long time."

"Yes," he said softly.

Her eyes returned to him.

And for one strange, suspended moment, she had the unsettling feeling he wasn't talking about the cemetery.

Then he stepped back smoothly.

"I am sure it has been a long day. You should rest."

Ember nodded once.

Right.

Rest.

Instead, she stood in her doorway, watching him cross the hall.

He opened the black-door of the apartment opposite hers and disappeared inside without another word.

The hallway fell silent.

But moments later, vinyl crackle drifted softly beneath his door.

Ember lingered there longer than she should have.

Listening.

You stand in the middle of the hallway, dripping rainwater onto century-old carpet while thunder rolls beyond the cemetery windows.

Your hair is damp against your throat.

Your pulse still uneven from carrying suitcases up four flights of stairs.

After watching your arrival from my balcony, I should have gone back inside and left you to your own devices.

Instead, I watch you laugh at your broken suitcase as though ruin has become familiar enough to amuse you.

You look exhausted.

You still smile anyway.

Interesting.

I hear the faint static scratch as the record continues spinning unattended in my apartment while you struggle with your key across the hall.

I reached for the handle of my apartment door, realizing that I left it unlocked.

I do not remember leaving my door unlocked.

That is unusual.

You turn once more toward the cemetery windows before stepping fully inside your apartment, and lightning illuminates your face in silver-white flashes.

For one impossible moment, the entire hallway narrows around you.

The building has housed artists.

Predators.

Collectors.

Women beautiful enough to start wars.

None of them arrested my attention the way you do standing there in wet black wool with rain trembling along your collarbone.

Ember.

The name suits you too well.

And when you look at me again from across the threshold of your apartment, I realize something uncomfortable.

I am already anticipating the next time your door opens.

Chapter 2

Handwritten Invitation

Ember discovered the envelope three nights after moving into Marceaux House.

By then, she had learned the building disliked mornings.

At dawn, the old pipes knocked behind the walls like someone trapped there, politely asking to be let out. The hallway sconces flickered without wind. The elevator remained out of order, though the handwritten cardboard sign had vanished and been replaced by a brass plaque engraved with the same message.

OUT OF ORDER.

No repair date.

No apology.

The building also disliked deliveries. Her grocery order had arrived downstairs and waited in the lobby beneath the suspicious regard of a marble saint missing one hand. The driver had refused to bring anything beyond the lobby, citing "bad reception" and "weird vibes" before fleeing into a sheet of New Orleans rain.

By the third day, Ember had accepted the stairs as penance for every questionable life decision she had made since nineteen.

She had also learned David Caesarius kept nocturnal hours.

Across the hall, his black door remained silent throughout daylight. No footsteps. No voices. No television murmuring through the wall. No clatter of dishes, or shower pipes, or phone calls. Nothing.

But after sunset, his apartment woke up .

Vinyl first.

Always vinyl.

Sometimes low violins, sometimes a woman singing in French, sometimes something darker and older, all bass pulse and mourning. The music never played loudly. It didn't need to. It seeped beneath his door and filled the hall with melancholy until Ember found herself lingering too long over the lock whenever she came home.

She told herself this was harmless.

People noticed music.

People noticed beautiful men across the hall with chilly hands and voices like candle smoke.

People noticed when those men looked at them as though they had interrupted the last two hundred years of their lives.

That was normal.

Probably.

On the third evening, she returned from the cemetery with rain beading on her coat and damp white roses still staining her fingertips.

The family crypt stood across the avenue next to a giant magnolia tree, its marble face streaked green with moss and age. Carved into the granite over the iron gate in stern block letters, the kind meant to outlast scandal, hurricanes, and descendants who forgot to visit, was the name GRANT.

Ember had not forgotten.

Not yet.

Her great-grandfather had left her the apartment, provided a small stipend if she lived there, and paid the taxes for ten years. Ten years. In New York, she had been counting quarters and deciding which bill could wait until the next panic attack. In New Orleans, a dead man had handed her walls, windows, a roof, and a cemetery view.

So, she brought him flowers.

White roses the first time because they were the only decent ones left at the corner shop. White roses the second time because the woman behind the counter had remembered her. White roses now, because ritual had its hooks in her already.

Rain followed her into the building.

The lobby smelled of wet stone and old candles. Someone had left a black umbrella standing in the brass holder near the mailboxes. It was long, elegant, and absurdly expensive-looking, with a silver handle shaped like a raven's head.

David's, probably.

No one else she had seen in the building seemed capable of owning such a theatrical object without irony.

Ember stopped at the mailboxes and checked hers out of habit.

Empty.

Of course.

She closed the small brass door and turned toward the stairs.

Finally arriving at the fourth-floor landing, she saw the envelope.

It waited on the floor before her apartment door, centered with such precision it seemed measured. Thick ivory paper. Heavy. Sealed with dark red wax.

For one bewildered second, Ember stood at the end of the fourth-floor hallway and stared.

The hall was quiet except for the rain tapping against the arched window behind her. David's door remained shut. No music tonight.

That unsettled her more than it should have.

She walked slowly toward the envelope.

Someone had written her name across the front in black ink.

Ember Grant.

Not printed.

Written.

Calligraphy curled around each letter with old-fashioned elegance, all controlled flourishes and sharp descenders. It looked less like an invitation than a summons.

Ember crouched and picked it up.

The paper felt cool against her damp fingers.

The wax seal bore no initials. Only a small, pressed image: a thorned rose wrapped around a crescent moon.

She glanced at David's door.

Black. Silent. Closed.

"Subtle," she murmured.

No answer.

Still, the back of her neck warmed.

Inside her apartment, the rooms were cold and blue with storm light. She had not unpacked much yet. Two suitcases lay open in her bedroom. Books sat in stacks on the floor instead of on shelves. Her sketchpads sat on the dining table beside an empty coffee cup, a box cutter, and a half-eaten sleeve of crackers.

Luxury it might be, but she could make it look desperate.

She locked the door behind her, shrugged out of her wet coat, and set the roses on the table. Her fingertips carried the green, crushed scent of stems.

The envelope remained in her other hand.

She should shower first.

Eat something.

Change socks.

Be practical for once in her life.

Instead, she slid one nail beneath the wax and opened the envelope with the reverence of a woman who knew some doors, once opened, changed the way a life was lived.

The card inside was thick, black stock.

Elegant White ink.

Handwritten.

Miss Grant,

I invite you to a private poetry reading this Friday evening at eight o'clock.

Apartment 4A.

I will provide wine, verse, and music.

Attendance is not mandatory.

It is, however, hoped for.

D. Caesarius

Ember read it once.

Then again.

Then, once more, because apparently she enjoyed making terrible decisions with her full attention.

Attendance is not mandatory.

It is, however, hoped for.

A laugh slipped out of her, soft and disbelieving.

"Who writes like this?"

The apartment offered no opinion.

Rain slid down the bay windows in long, trembling lines. Beyond the glass, the cemetery blurred beneath the storm. The crypts stood pale and solemn across the avenue, white roses dim at her great-grandfather's gate.

Ember carried the invitation to the window.

Apartment 4A.

Across the hall.

David Caesarius.

She had only spoken to him once, unless "thank you" and "that seems unfair" counted as a meaningful relationship. Since then, she had seen him twice.

Once from the lobby, where he stood near the mailboxes, speaking quietly to a woman in a black velvet coat. The woman had laughed at something he said, leaned too close, and gone silent the moment Ember entered. David had turned his head immediately.

Not toward the sound.

Toward Ember.

As if he had already known the precise second she would appear.

The second time had been through the bay window.

Or rather, she had seen his reflection in the dark glass while she unpacked books near midnight.

He had been standing on his balcony next to the narrow angle of the hall window, smoke drifting from one hand, his dark figure framed against the wet iron railing.

Watching the cemetery.

She had told herself he was watching the cemetery.

She looked down at the invitation.

Wine, verse, and music.

Danger wore elegant stationery now.

That was new.

Her phone buzzed on the table, startling her so badly that the card snapped against her palm.

A text from a former coworker in Brooklyn.

Did you make it to spooky inheritance manor alive?

Ember stared at it, smiled despite herself, and typed:

Define alive.

Three dots appeared.

Then: *That bad?*

Ember glanced around the apartment. High ceilings. Damp windows. Old, but luxurious furniture throughout the large, open rooms. An invitation from a beautiful man across the hall who wrote like Lord Byron learned manners from a funeral director.

She typed: *Weird. Beautiful. Possibly haunted. Jury still out.*

Her friend replied with a skull emoji, a heart, and:

Do NOT sleep with the first hot gothic man you meet.

Ember looked toward the closed front door.

Too late to rule it out philosophically.

She deleted three possible replies and instead sent:

I have standards.

Another buzz.

No, you have gothic aesthetics. Different disease.

Ember laughed.

A knock sounded at her door.

Not loud.

Not urgent.

Two soft taps.

Her smile vanished.

The phone lay in her hand, screen glowing. Outside, thunder rolled over the cemetery, low and slow.

Another knock.

One tap this time.

As if the person outside knew she already stood near enough to hear.

Placing her phone back down on the table, Ember crossed the apartment quietly, though the old floorboards betrayed her every step. She checked the peephole.

David Caesarius stood in the hallway.

Of course he did.

Black dress shirt. Dark trousers. No coat tonight. His dark hair was damp, swept back from his face as if he had walked through rain and cared nothing for it. In one hand, he held a bottle of red wine by the neck.

No umbrella.

No nervousness.

No visible concern over appearing at her door moments after she opened his invitation.

Ember unlocked the door and opened it halfway.

David's gaze dropped first to her hand.

To the black card.

Then rose to her face.

"You found it," he said.

"You left it in front of my door."

"Yes."

She waited.

He did not elaborate.

"Is that something you do often?"

"Leave invitations?"

"Handwritten invitations sealed with wax and ominous botanical symbolism."

His mouth curved faintly.

"Only for neighbors worth alarming."

She should not have enjoyed that.

She did.

The hallway lights flickered once. Gold shifted over his cheekbones, catching the silver ring on his index finger.

Ember leaned one shoulder against the doorframe. "You could have just asked."

"I considered it."

"And?"

"You had gone to the cemetery." His gaze moved past her for half a breath, toward the roses on her table. "I did not want to interrupt."

Everything in her went still.

Not frightened.

Not yet.

Aware.

"You saw me?"

"Yes."

The answer came without hesitation.

No awkwardness.

No scramble.

No fake coincidence.

Just yes.

"From your window?"

"From the balcony."

"Do you make a habit of watching women in cemeteries, Mr. Caesarius?"

"No."

His eyes held hers.

A pause entered the hallway and settled there, warm as breath.

"Only you."

The words should have sounded ridiculous. Too direct. Too much. Something from a man who wore too much cologne in a hotel bar.

From David, they sounded almost factual.

Worse.

They sounded intimate.

Ember tightened her grip on the door.

"Do you think that answer improves the situation?"

"It clarifies it."

"It certainly does."

His gaze lowered to her mouth. Not long. Long enough.

Then back to her eyes.

"I can apologize if you prefer."

"Would you mean it?"

"No."

She laughed once, helplessly.

That faint curve touched his mouth again, and this time she understood the danger of it. He did not smile often enough. When he did, the entire hallway changed temperature.

"You're honest," she said.

"When useful."

"And is honesty useful right now?"

"I hope so."

Rain whispered against the far window at the end of the hall.

David lifted the wine bottle slightly.

"A peace offering."

"For watching me in the cemetery?"

"For alarming you with botanical symbolism."

"That's a niche offense."

"I specialize."

His voice remained quiet, but something beneath it warmed. Not playfulness exactly. David did not seem like a playful man.

But he liked this.

The realization slipped through Ember with the dangerous sweetness of wine on an empty stomach.

He liked speaking with her.

He liked standing at her threshold.

He liked that she did not retreat.

She looked at the bottle. "Is that for tonight or Friday?"

"Tonight, if you accept it. Friday, if you refuse it tonight."

"You came prepared for both outcomes?"

"I prefer not to rely on chance."

"No? You seem like a man who enjoys theatrics."

"Theatrics are most effective when carefully managed."

Her eyes narrowed. "That sounds like something a villain says before revealing a trapdoor."

"Do you see a trapdoor?"

"In this building? I'm not ruling anything out."

The almost-smile returned.

Then faded into something more focused as his gaze drifted over her shoulder into the apartment.

Not rudely.

Not intrusively.

As if he were checking whether the rooms had accepted her yet.

"You are settling in," he said.

"Is that a polite way of saying I live out of suitcases and boxes?"

"It is an observation."

"You make a lot of those?"

"Yes."

Again, no shame.

No disguise.

Her pulse beat once, harder than before.

David's eyes flicked to her throat.

Ember noticed.

His fingers tightened around the wine bottle.

Only slightly.

But she saw it.

And there it was again, that strange, impossible impression: beneath all his stillness, something waited with its teeth closed.

She should step back.

She should thank him for the invitation, take the wine, close the door, and call her friend in Brooklyn to announce that the hot gothic neighbor was indeed a problem.

Instead, she asked, "Did you write it yourself?"

His eyes returned to hers.

"The invitation?"

"The calligraphy."

"Yes."

"You're good."

"I have had practice."

"At inviting strange women from across the hall?"

"At writing beautifully."

There was arrogance in that answer.

Soft arrogance.

The kind worn close to the skin.

Ember liked that too.

God help her.

She turned the card over in her hand, tracing the edge with her thumb. "Why a poetry reading?"

"Because poetry reveals people faster than conversation does."

"That sounds dangerous."

"It can be."

"And you host these often?"

David looked at her for a long second.

"No."

A small shiver moved down her spine.

He noticed that, too.

She was beginning to suspect David Caesarius noticed everything.

"How often?" she asked.

"Rarely."

"How rarely?"

His voice lowered.

"This will be the first in some time."

The hallway seemed to shrink around them.

Ember's apartment waited behind her, cold and half-unpacked. His door waited across the hall, black and silent. Between them, rain, brass light, and an invitation written by hand.

"You invited other people, right?"

"Yes."

"That hesitation is not comforting."

"It was not hesitation. I was deciding how much truth to offer."

Her mouth went dry.

"And?"

"The reading is real. The guests are real. The wine is real."

"But?"

His gaze settled on the invitation in her hand.

"But I wrote that invitation for you."

Oh.

There it was.

No flourish.

No seduction pressed thick over the words.

Just a silent blade slid between her ribs.

Ember's fingers curled around the card.

Outside, thunder cracked sharp enough to make the sconces flicker.

David did not flinch.

Neither did she, which seemed to please him.

"Why?" she asked.

"For the same reason I helped with your suitcase."

"You felt sorry for me?"

"No."

His answer came too quickly for politeness.

Something in his expression sharpened, and for one breath, Ember glimpsed what his calm concealed.

Not kindness.

Not loneliness.

Hunger given manners.

"You caught my attention," he said.

Silence.

The rain thickened.

"That's all?" she asked.

"No." His gaze moved over her face slowly, so slowly her skin warmed beneath it. "But it is where I am willing to begin."

Ember could not remember the last time a man had looked at her without rushing toward whatever he wanted from her.

David did not rush.

He stood outside her apartment with wine in one hand and patience in every line of his body, and somehow that patience felt more indecent than urgency.

She ought to be irritated.

Part of her was.

Another part wanted to know what he would do if she stepped closer.

That part had poor survival instincts.

"Friday at eight," she said, because she needed words and those were available.

"Yes."

"What should I bring?"

"Yourself."

"Smooth."

"Accurate."

She laughed again, quieter now.

David's gaze softened by a fraction. "And if you own something black..."

"I own many things black."

"I suspected."

"Is there a dress code?"

"No." A pause. "But I would like to see what you choose."

The words moved through her like fingertips along the back of her neck.

She looked away first.

Not because she wanted to.

Because she had to.

"Wine," she said, holding out her hand.

David offered the bottle.

Their fingers touched around the glass.

Cold again.

This time, Ember didn't pull away.

Neither did he.

The bottle remained suspended between them, his hand above hers, his silver pinky ring brushing her knuckle. The contact was minor. Absurdly minor.

Her body disagreed.

David looked down at their hands.

His lashes lowered.

For the first time since she'd met him, he seemed less composed.

Not much.

A hairline fracture in marble.

"You are still cold from the cemetery," he said.

"I'm fine."

"You say that as if it answers anything."

"It answers enough."

"No." His thumb shifted against her knuckle, slow enough to be deniable. "It does not."

Her breath caught.

His gaze lifted.

There was no smile now.

Only attention.

Deep.

Unblinking.

Absolute.

Ember understood with sudden, vivid clarity that David had not come to her door because of the invitation.

The invitation had been paper.

This was the true summons.

The hallway.

The rain.

The wine.

The first touch neither of them had ended.

Across the corridor, something old groaned within the walls of Marceaux House.

David released the bottle first.

"Friday, then," he said.

Ember held the wine against her chest. "Friday."

He stepped back.

The distance should have helped.

It did not.

At his door, he paused and turned.

"One more thing, Miss Grant."

She hated how that sounded in his voice.

Loved it too.

"What?"

"When you come over..."

His gaze dipped to the invitation in her hand.

"Do not knock."

Her eyebrows rose. "No?"

"No."

"Why?"

His hand settled on the knob of his black door.

"Because I will know when you arrive."

Then he opened his apartment and disappeared inside.

A heartbeat later, music began.

Vinyl crackle first.

Then a low cello, dark and intimate, threading beneath the rain.

Ember stood in her doorway with his wine in one hand and his invitation in the other, wondering when exactly she had stopped being afraid of strange things and started wanting them to request her by name.

YOU READ MY INVITATION three times.

I hear the shift in your breathing through the wall before you laugh.

Soft.

Disbelieving.

Not afraid enough.

Not yet.

The day-old roses you carried home from the cemetery sit on your table, white petals bruised by rain. Your fingers smell of stems, wet stone, and the faint metallic edge of old iron from the crypt gate.

You do not know how strongly humans carry ritual on their skin.

Grief has a scent.

Gratitude too.

Yours is stranger.

Warmer.

You stand by your window with my card in your hand, and I imagine your thumb moving over the letters of your name.

Ember Grant.

I wrote it slowly.

More slowly than necessary.

Ink rewards patience.

So do women who do not startle when watched.

When I knock, your pulse jumps before your footsteps cross the room. By the time you open the door, you have already decided to pretend calm.

Beautiful effort.

Useless, but beautiful.

You challenge me about the cemetery, as if I should be ashamed of noticing you among the dead.

I am not.

You stood before that crypt in the rain with white roses in your hands, thanking a dead man for giving you shelter.

Most people beg the living for rescue.

You thanked the dead.

Do you understand how arresting that is?

No.

Not yet.

You will.

You ask why I wrote the invitation.

I tell you only the smallest truth.

That you caught my attention.

Not that I watched from my balcony the first evening as you arrived soaked and furious with the weeping sky.

Not that I remember the exact sound of your laugh when the suitcase broke.

Not that the hallway has seemed offensively silent since your door closed.

Not that I have thought of your throat each time music begins.

Those truths require candlelight.

Wine.

A room full of witnesses who will not save you.

Friday will do.

When our fingers touch around the bottle, you do not pull away.

I admire that more than I should.

Your skin is warm.

Alive!

Startlingly alive.

For one moment, I consider stepping closer. Taking your chin. Testing whether your mouth tastes like rain, roses, or defiance.

Instead, I release you.

Restraint is not mercy.

It is preparation.

You stand there holding what I gave you, eyes too bright in the hall light, and I tell you not to knock when you come to me.

You ask why.

Because I will know when you arrive.

Because I will hear your footsteps.

Because I will smell rain in your hair before your hand reaches my door.

Because Ember, I invited several guests to a poetry reading.

But you are the reason the candles will be lit.

Chapter 3
Rain Against Glass

Friday arrived beneath rain.

Not the violent storm that had greeted Ember on her first night in New Orleans. This rain drifted softer through the city, steady and silver against the cemetery gates. It glossed the crypts in muted pearl and turned the streets outside Marceaux House reflective enough to resemble drowned mirrors.

Ember stood in front of her bedroom mirror, holding three black dresses hostage against indecision.

“This is absurd,” she informed her reflection.

Her reflection offered no useful counsel.

The invitation lay open on the bed behind her, beside David’s bottle of wine, now half empty from the previous evening. She had intended to save it. Instead, she’d poured a single glass while unpacking books and somehow found herself drinking alone beside the cemetery windows while cello music drifted faintly through the wall from Apartment 4A.

The experience had felt dangerously close to intimacy.

Which was ridiculous.

She barely knew him.

Granted, she had also spent the day thinking about the exact way his thumb had shifted against her knuckle in the hallway.

But that was beside the point.

Probably.

She selected the black dress with the lowest neckline and immediately resented herself for it.

The fabric clung softly without looking overtly provocative. Long sleeves. Thin material. A silver chain rested against her collarbone, almost disappearing briefly between her breasts before reemerging lower against the dark fabric.

Subtle.

Mostly.

Her hair fell loose tonight, dark auburn waves spilling over bare shoulders. She lined her eyes in charcoal, added lipstick darker than she usually wore, then stared at herself again.

"You are dressing for a poetry reading," she muttered.

Not a seduction ritual hosted by a vampire-shaped problem across the hall.

Thunder rolled softly beyond the windows.

Too late now.

At precisely eight o'clock, Ember stepped into the hallway.

And stopped.

David's door already stood open.

Warm amber light spilled across the corridor in flickering gold. Music drifted outward immediately. Not cello tonight. Something older. Slow piano beneath the hiss of vinyl static.

And beneath it all: voices.

Low.

Elegant.

Laughing softly.

Waiting.

Ember's pulse quickened.

The hallway smelled faintly of candle wax, expensive wine, smoke, and rain carried in on damp coats.

No one appeared in the doorway to greet her.

For one suspended second, she remembered his words.

Do not knock.

Because I will know when you arrive.

Then David appeared from somewhere deeper inside the apartment.

And every coherent thought abandoned her without notice.

Black dress shirt.

Sleeves rolled once at the forearms.

No jacket tonight.

The open collar revealed a glimpse of pale throat beneath candlelight, while silver rings flashed briefly as he rested one hand against the dark wood frame of the door.

His eyes found her instantly.

Not casually.

Not socially.

Hungrily.

The entire apartment seemed to fall quieter around that look.

David said nothing at first.

His gaze crawled from her shoes upward, taking in the dress, her throat, her mouth, the loose fall of her hair.

When his eyes returned to hers, something dark flickered there.

Approval.

Strong enough to feel physical.

"You came," he said softly.

Ember hated how much she enjoyed hearing that.

"You sounded confident I would."

"I was."

"That seems arrogant."

"It was observant."

His gaze dipped once more to the neckline of her dress.

Then lingered.

Not long enough to insult.

Long enough to unsettle.

"Black suits you," he murmured.

The warmth rushing into her face irritated her immediately.

"You're staring."

"Yes."

No embarrassment.

No retreat.

No apology.

Just yes.

Ember exhaled sharply through her nose. "You know, most people learn to disguise that impulse."

"Most people are cowards."

His mouth curved faintly at whatever expression crossed her face.

Then he stepped aside.

"Come in, Ember."

The apartment beyond him glowed like something removed from ordinary time.

Candles flickered everywhere.

Tall black tapers burned beside towering bookshelves and low velvet furniture. Rain streaked the massive cemetery-facing windows while shadows shifted lazily across dark wallpaper and antique paintings.

Vinyl spun slowly near the fireplace.

The guests turned toward her almost immediately.

Not all at once.

That would have felt staged.

But gradually.

Like flowers bending toward warmth.

Ember became sharply aware of herself beneath those gazes.

There were six guests in total.

Three men.

Three women.

Beautiful in unsettling ways.

Too elegant.

Too still.

Too attentive.

A pale blond man lounged beside the fireplace with one ankle crossed over his knee, a crystal glass dangling lazily from long fingers. His silver-blond hair fell almost white beneath candlelight.

He looked Ember over once and smiled without warmth.

Interesting.

Beside him sat a woman in black velvet with blood-red lipstick and silver rosary beads wound around one wrist. Her dark eyes lingered on Ember thoughtfully.

The remaining guests offered quieter greetings.

Wine was pressed into Ember's hand by a dark-skinned man in gold-rimmed glasses whose rich brown eyes seemed almost kind compared to the others.

"Lucien Roptera," he introduced himself smoothly. "You are causing quite a disturbance already."

Ember blinked. "Excuse me?"

Lucien's smile deepened slightly. "David cleaned his apartment twice today."

From near the fireplace, the blond vampire laughed softly into his glass.

David did not look embarrassed.

He looked annoyed.

"Lucien," he said calmly.

"My apologies," Lucien replied without sounding sorry at all.

Ember glanced toward David.

"You cleaned for me?"

His gaze settled on her with unnerving steadiness.

"Yes."

God.

Everything with him sounded too intimate.

Before she could recover, the blond man rose from his chair and approached.

Tall.

Elegant.

Predatory.

His pale blue eyes moved over Ember with open curiosity.

"Adrien Avenoire," he introduced. "And before you ask, yes. He has been insufferable all week."

"Adrien," David warned quietly.

Adrien ignored him completely.

"You should feel honored," he continued. "David rarely notices anyone long enough to become unbearable about them."

Ember looked between them carefully.

David stood near enough behind Adrien that the room itself seemed to tighten around his silence.

Not anger exactly.

Possession.

And suddenly Ember understood something instinctively: these people knew what David's attention meant.

Better than she did.

The realization sent heat down her spine.

Adrien smiled slowly as if he saw the exact moment understanding touched her.

Dangerous man.

Dangerous room.

Dangerous decision wearing lipstick and pretending to be social curiosity.

Ember took a long sip of wine.

"Good to know I inspire psychological decline."

Adrien laughed genuinely this time.

David's eyes remained on Ember over the rim of his own glass.

"You do," he said quietly.

The room fell silent for one heartbeat too long.

Then Lucien lifted his glass lazily. "Well," he drawled. "This is either the beginning of a great romance or an exceptionally beautiful disaster."

"Both are acceptable outcomes," Adrien murmured.

David never looked away from Ember.

"Yes," he said softly.

"They are."

LATER, THE POETRY BEGAN.

Candles burned lower by then.

Rain moved steadily beyond the windows while guests settled throughout the apartment with wineglasses and loose-limbed elegance. Ember sat near the enormous bay window overlooking the cemetery, velvet cushions beneath her while lightning flashed silver over marble crypts outside.

David remained standing near the fireplace.

Watching her.

Always watching her.

One of the women read first. Then Lucien. Then Adrien offered something decadent and cruel in French that made his companion smile into her wineglass.

But the room changed when David finally stepped forward.

The shift was immediate.

Subtle.

Absolute.

Conversation ceased.

Even the rain seemed quieter.

David held no book in his hands.

No paper.

Of course he didn't.

A man like him would memorize poetry before permitting himself to read it aloud.

His eyes found Ember immediately.

Then stayed there.

The poem began softly.

"Some people enter a room
the way candles surrender flame.
Quietly.
Without understanding
they have altered the shape of the dark."

No one moved.

Not even Ember.

David's voice wrapped itself around the room like velvet smoke.

"I had forgotten distraction.
Forgotten the humiliation of wanting to look twice.
Then you arrived, rain-soaked and furious,
dragging ruined luggage behind you
like a woman surviving the end of a city."

A pulse beat hard beneath Ember's throat.

No one else in the room reacted with surprise.

That frightened her more than the poem itself.

They knew.

They all knew this was for her.

David continued.

"You stood before the dead with white roses in your hands
and thanked them for shelter.
Do you understand what that did to me?"

The candlelight flickered across his face.

Beautiful.

Still.

Terrifyingly intent.

"I think some people are born carrying storms inside them.
Others become storms slowly.
You..."

His gaze lowered briefly to her mouth.

"...you arrived as one."

Ember forgot her wineglass existed.

Forgot the room.

Forgot the guests.

There was only his voice and the unbearable sensation of being seen too clearly.

The poem softened.

Dangerously.

"And now the building waits for your footsteps.
The hallway listens when you return home.
Even the records sound different after midnight."

A faint smile touched his mouth then.

Small.

Private.

"As do I."

Silence flooded the apartment afterward.

Not awkward silence.

Reverent silence.

The kind that follows a confession.

Ember realized slowly that her fingers had tightened around her wineglass hard enough to ache.

Across the room, Adrien watched her with open amusement.

Lucien looked almost sympathetic.

And David...

David looked satisfied.

As though he had revealed exactly as much as he intended.

No more.

No less.

The rain deepened outside.

Then Adrien broke the silence smoothly by lifting his glass.

"To obsession," he toasted lazily.

A few soft laughs rippled through the room.

David never looked away from Ember.

"To attention," he corrected quietly.

The words moved through her like fingers beneath silk.

And for the first time since arriving at Marceaux House, Ember understood something with terrifying certainty.

David Caesarius had not invited her to a poetry reading.

He had invited witnesses.

Chapter 4
Vinyl & Candlelight

The last guests left sometime after one in the morning.

Ember tracked their departures by fragments.

Adrien Avenoire lifting his date, Thessa Rigby's hand to his mouth with mocking elegance before leading her toward the door. Lucien Roptera pausing beside the record player to exchange a look with David that felt weighted with private meaning. Candlelight flickering across velvet coats and silver jewelry as the apartment slowly emptied itself of beautiful people and their willing companions.

Rain whispered steadily beyond the cemetery windows.

And through it all, David watched Ember.

Not constantly.

Constantly would have felt easier somehow.

Instead, his attention returned to her in measured intervals, each glance deliberate enough to leave warmth beneath her skin long after it passed.

By the time the front door finally closed behind Lucien, the apartment had fallen almost unnaturally quiet.

Vinyl crackled softly near the fireplace.

Candles burned lower now, their wax spilling down black tapers like melted ink.

Ember stood near the enormous bay window with her wineglass cradled loosely in one hand while lightning flashed silver over the cemetery below.

The crypts looked submerged tonight.

Like Atlantis for the dead.

"You're thinking too loudly."

David's voice drifted toward her from across the room.

Ember glanced over one shoulder.

He stood near the dining table, collecting abandoned glasses with infuriating composure, black sleeves still rolled to his forearms. The candlelight sharpened the elegant planes of his face into something almost unreal.

"You can hear thinking now?" she asked.

"I can hear yours."

"That's concerning."

"Yes."

The answer came too smoothly to be reassuring.

Ember laughed softly and turned back toward the windows.

The rain blurred the cemetery gates into streaks of black iron and silver water. Somewhere in the distance, thunder rolled low through the city.

Behind her, crystal touched wood softly as David set another glass aside.

"You handled them well tonight," he said.

"The beautiful vampires or their human companions?"

A pause.

"All of them."

Ember smiled faintly into her wine.

"So, you are telling me they are vampires."

She felt, rather than saw, his stillness behind her.

Interesting.

"I did not say that."

"No," she agreed. "But you also didn't correct me."

David crossed the room slowly enough for her to hear each step against the hardwood floor.

When he stopped beside her at the window, his reflection appeared beside hers in the darkened glass.

Tall.

Black-clad.

Pale beneath candlelight.

Beautiful enough to feel dangerous.

"If you thought they were vampires ... You weren't frightened," he observed.

"Should I have been?"

"Around vampires? Most people would have been."

Ember considered that honestly.

Maybe she should have been.

The room had contained too many still people. Too many sharp smiles. Too much eye contact lingering a fraction too long.

And yet—

"No," she admitted softly. "Not frightened."

David's gaze moved to her reflection in the window.

"What did you feel?"

The question settled beneath her ribs strangely.

Not casual curiosity.

Focused interest.

Like he genuinely wanted the answer.

Ember traced one fingertip slowly around the stem of her wineglass.

"Observed."

The corner of his mouth shifted faintly.

"Yes."

"There's that honesty again."

"You dislike it?"

"No." She looked toward him finally. "I think I dislike how much you enjoy it."

Something dark flickered briefly behind his eyes.

Not amusement.

Recognition.

"Fair."

Lightning flashed outside.

For one sharp instant, the cemetery illuminated in silver-white detail below them. Marble angels. Iron fencing. Rain streaming down crypt walls.

Ember exhaled softly.

"I still can't believe this is real."

"The apartment?"

"The whole thing." She gestured vaguely toward the windows, the building, the storm outside. "A month ago, I was arguing with city inspectors while my apartment ceiling collapsed into my bathtub."

David turned slightly toward her.

"You lived alone in New York?"

"Yes."

"And now?"

"I live across from a man who hosts gothic poetry readings with people who pretend to be 'vampires'."

"You say that as though it's unfortunate."

"It remains under review."

That earned another almost-smile.

God.

Those smiles were becoming addictive.

David rested one hand lightly against the window frame beside her. Long fingers. Silver rings catching candlelight.

"You miss New York," he said.

Not a question.

Ember stared out at the rain.

"Sometimes."

"Not enough to return."

"Without a job or money, returning would be foolish. So, no."

That answer came too quickly.

David noticed.

Of course, he noticed.

"What do you miss?" he asked quietly.

The question should not have sounded intimate.

It did anyway.

Ember leaned one shoulder lightly against the wall beside the bay window.

"The noise," she admitted. "The feeling that something was always happening somewhere. Delis at three in the morning. Sirens. Crowded trains. Terrible coffee that somehow tasted comforting because someone handed it to you through bulletproof glass."

David listened without interruption.

No fake sympathy.

No reassuring noises.

No interruption at all.

Just attention.

Which somehow felt more intimate than comfort.

"But I don't miss struggling there," she admitted after a moment. "Toward the end, I was exhausted all the time. I stopped drawing. I stopped sleeping properly. Every conversation, every thought, became about money."

David's gaze remained steady on her face.

"You are still exhausted."

The quiet certainty in his voice unsettled her more than concern would have.

"You say that as if you've been studying me."

"I have."

Ember's pulse stumbled once.

There it was again.

That impossible directness.

No shame.

No hesitation.

Just truth sharpened into intimacy.

"You admit things most people would hide," she murmured.

"Most people waste time pretending their intentions are mysterious."

"And yours aren't?"

"No."

Lightning flashed again.

This time, neither of them looked toward the cemetery.

Ember became aware suddenly of how close he stood beside her.

Not touching.

Not quite.

But near enough that she could smell wine, dark fabric, clove smoke, something colder beneath it all

"You make honesty sound dangerous," she said softly.

"It usually is."

The room quieted around them.

The record continued spinning somewhere behind them, low piano drifting beneath the rain.

David studied her with that same unbearable attentiveness he'd worn all evening.

Not merely looking.

Absorbing.

Ember's skin warmed beneath it.

"You never answered Lucien's question," she said finally.

"Which one?"

"Whether this is the beginning of a romance or a disaster."

His gaze lowered briefly to her mouth.

Then returned upward.

"I believe," he said carefully, "those things are often indistinguishable at first."

The answer slid through her slowly.

Like velvet dragged over sharpened steel.

Outside, thunder rolled softly across the cemetery.

Ember turned back toward the window before she did something profoundly unwise, like step closer to him.

Below them, rainwater streamed down marble crypts in silver ribbons. The Grant family mausoleum stood partially obscured beneath the magnolia tree, pale against the storm.

David followed her gaze immediately.

"You visit often," he observed.

"Three times this week isn't often."

"It is for someone your age."

Ember glanced toward him again. "What does that mean?"

"Most people avoid cemeteries unless forced."

"I'm grateful to him."

"Your great-grandfather."

"Yes."

The candlelight flickered softly across David's face as he watched the crypt below.

"You bring white roses every time."

Ember went still.

Slowly, she looked toward him.

"You noticed that."

"Yes."

"How?"

His eyes shifted to hers.

"I notice what matters to me."

The answer entered her bloodstream too quickly.

Dangerously quickly.

Ember set her wineglass carefully onto the nearby windowsill before she dropped it.

"You say things like that very casually."

"Would you prefer I lied?"

"No," she admitted quietly.

David stepped closer then.

Only half a step.

Still not touching.

But close enough now that she could feel the strange absence of warmth radiating from him.

Cold.

Not unpleasant.

Just unnatural.

"You arrange the flowers before you leave," he continued softly. "Most people place them carelessly."

Ember stared at him.

"How long have you been watching me?"

The question hung between them.

David considered her silently for one measured breath.

"Since the first evening."

Rain bolted against the windows suddenly.

The candle flames shifted.

Ember should have felt alarmed.

Instead, heat crawled through her stomach.

Because he wasn't lying.

Because every terrible, intimate thing he said arrived wrapped in absolute sincerity.

"And what exactly," she asked carefully, "made me so interesting?"

David's gaze moved over her face slowly enough to feel physical.

"Everything."

The word settled low in her body.

Too low.

Her pulse beat harder beneath her throat.

David's eyes flicked toward it instantly.

There.

Just for a second.

Something changed in him.

Not visibly.

Felt.

Like a predator lifting its head after catching a scent.

The shift vanished almost immediately beneath composure.

But Ember saw it.

And suddenly the room felt smaller.

Quieter.

More dangerous.

David seemed to realize she had noticed.

A strange stillness entered him then.

Controlled.

Measured.

Tightened beneath the skin.

"Forgive me," he said quietly.

The apology startled her.

"You're apologizing?"

"For staring."

Ember swallowed once.

"You've done a lot of that tonight."

"Yes."

Again: honest.

Always honest.

David lowered his gaze briefly toward the cemetery before speaking again.

"I find you difficult to ignore."

The candlelight trembled softly between them.

And Ember understood with growing, dangerous clarity that David Caesarius was not flirting the way ordinary men flirted.

Ordinary men performed attraction.

David observed it.

Catalogued it.

Spoke it aloud with terrifying calm.

Like desire was simply another fact worth stating.

The realization made her heart beat harder.

Which only seemed to worsen the problem.

Because his eyes returned once more to her throat.

This time, lingering.

Not long.

Long enough.

Then the record player clicked softly behind them.

The song had ended.

Neither of them moved.

Neither restarted it.

The silence stretched warm and strange between them while rain slid endlessly down the glass and the crypts of the cemetery.

And slowly, horrifyingly, Ember realized David had probably stopped hearing the music long before she had.

Chapter 5

The Architecture of Silence

Ember lasted until Sunday night before she did something foolish.

That sounded better than admitting she had spent all of Saturday listening for David's door.

Saturday had been a study in avoidance. She unpacked the kitchen boxes that had finally arrived. Rearranged books. Discovered the apartment came with three sets of chipped china, six tarnished candlesticks, and a locked writing desk in the bedroom with no key. She washed laundry in the narrow utility closet, burned toast, and pretended not to notice each time silence gathered too heavily across the hall.

No vinyl.

No footsteps.

No low masculine voice murmuring through the wood.

Nothing.

By eleven o'clock, she had stood beside her front door with a glass of water in hand for a full minute before realizing she had no reason to be there.

"This is pathetic," she told the lock.

The lock, old and brass and loyal to Marceaux House, offered no defense.

Sunday proved worse because rain returned before dusk.

It began as mist over the cemetery, turning the marble crypts soft-edged and ghostly beneath the streetlamps. By seven, the drizzle thickened into steady silver threads falling past Ember's bay windows. By eight, she had changed into black leggings and an oversized sweater, brewed coffee too late in the evening, and opened her sketchbook for the first time in weeks.

The page stayed blank.

Across the hall, vinyl crackled to life.

Ember froze.

It was absurd how fast her body responded. Her hand tightened around the pencil. Her pulse lifted. Every room in her apartment seemed to lean toward that faint sound.

A slow guitar entered first.

Then more strings.

Then a woman's voice, smoky and low, singing as though heartbreak had poured itself into a glass and learned melody.

Ember set the pencil down.

"No," she said softly.

The music continued.

Of course it did.

She tried to ignore it for ten minutes.

At eleven, she made the mistake of walking to her door.

At twelve, she opened it.

The hallway glowed with a low amber light. Rain tapped against the arched window at the far end. David's black door stood closed, but music slipped beneath it like a secret.

Ember stared at the floor.

She could knock.

She should not knock.

He had told her not to knock on Friday, but Friday had been an invitation. This was Sunday. Entirely different species of bad judgment.

She turned to go back inside.

His door opened.

David stood there with one hand on the knob, dressed in black trousers and a charcoal shirt open at the throat. No shoes. No coat. Dark hair slightly disordered, as if he had been reading, or brooding, or doing whatever beautiful, impossible men did alone after sunset in apartments full of candles and old records.

His gaze dropped to her bare feet.

Then rose slowly.

"You were leaving," he said.

"I was never here."

"Unconvincing."

"I've been told I need to work on subtlety."

"Yes."

His mouth did not smile, but his eyes warmed with something dangerously close to amusement.

Behind him, the record continued to spin.

Ember folded her arms. “Your music is loud.”

“No, it isn’t.”

“No,” she admitted. “But it’s distracting.”

That did earn the faint curve of his mouth.

“Good.”

“You’re insufferable.”

“So, Adrien has mentioned.”

“He seems perceptive.”

“He is unbearable when encouraged.”

“Most men are.”

David looked at her for one silent beat.

Then said, “Would you like to come in?”

That was the problem with David Caesarius. He made terrible decisions sound elegantly reasonable.

Ember glanced past him into the apartment.

The lights were lower tonight. Only a few candles burned near the bookshelves and beside the record player. Rain streaked the cemetery windows beyond, drawing watery lines through the reflected candlelight. His apartment smelled faintly of clove smoke, wine, old paper, and something cool beneath it all.

No guests.

No witnesses.

No convenient audience to dilute the weight of his attention.

“I shouldn’t,” she said.

“No.”

Her eyebrows rose. “That was your cue to persuade me.”

“I dislike persuading women to enter my apartment.”

That should not have pleased her.

It did.

“So, you’re leaving it to my poor judgment?”

“Entirely.”

His voice lowered by half a shade.

“I trust it brought you to my door for a reason.”

Heat rose beneath her skin.

Ember looked away first, toward the rain-glossed hallway window.

"I wanted to know what song this was."

David stepped back, opening the door wider.

"Then come and learn."

A sensible woman would have declined.

Ember had never claimed to be sensible.

She crossed the threshold.

The moment she entered, the room seemed to close around her with velvet patience. It was quieter than it had been Friday, stripped of laughter and conversation. Without other bodies, David's apartment became more intimate. More itself.

Books everywhere. Dark walls. Heavy curtains. Framed sketches and old photographs. A fireplace unlit but stacked with wood as though flame remained an option. The bay windows looked down over the cemetery, rain blurring the crypts until they seemed to float beneath black water.

Near the fireplace stood the record player.

Not modern.

A large wooden console, polished dark as old blood, its brass details gleaming under candlelight. Beside it, shelves climbed almost to the ceiling, packed with vinyl in careful rows. Some sleeves looked new. Others were worn soft at the corners, their colors faded by age and handling.

Ember drifted toward them despite herself.

"This is not a record collection," she said.

"No?"

"This is a symptom."

David closed the door behind her. The soft click of the latch moved through her spine.

"Of what?"

"Obsession, probably."

"Probably," he agreed.

She glanced over her shoulder.

He watched her from beside the door, perfectly still.

"You're not defending yourself?"

"Against accuracy?"

"Fair."

The current record played low and mournful, the singer's voice almost swallowed by the rain.

Ember crouched near the shelves, careful not to touch yet.

"You organize alphabetically?"

"Sometimes."

"That is not an answer."

"It depends on the year."

"Of release?"

"Of acquisition."

She looked back at him. "That is a concerningly romantic way to organize records."

"Music remembers when it entered a life."

The line was beautiful enough to irritate her.

"You say things like that on purpose."

"Yes."

"At least you admit it."

"I have found denial tedious."

Ember turned back to the shelves before his gaze did worse things to her breathing.

The records were exquisite. Darkwave. Classical. Jazz. Blues. Spoken poetry. French chansons. Old opera. Obscure goth bands she recognized only because one of her college roommates had spent sophomore year dressing like a haunted widow and educating everyone against their will.

Then her fingers stopped on a worn black sleeve.

"No way."

David's voice came closer. "You know that one."

She pulled the record free carefully. "My mother used to play this when she painted."

"A painter?"

"For a while. She became an accountant after my father left."

"A brutal transition."

"Not for her. She liked numbers. Said they behaved better than men."

David's quiet laugh moved over the back of her neck.

Ember realized he stood behind her now.

Not touching.

Close enough for awareness.

Close enough for trouble.

She looked down at the record to avoid turning into his chest like a moth into black flame.

"She played it on Sundays," Ember said. "Loudly. Windows open. Coffee burning. Paint everywhere. She'd tell me this album made loneliness sound expensive."

David leaned slightly beside her, reaching toward the shelf above her shoulder.

His arm passed near her face.

No contact.

The absence of it somehow worse.

"She had taste," he said.

"She had chaos."

"The two often share a room."

He drew out another record, glanced at the cover, and set it aside.

Ember held the worn album carefully between both hands. "May I?"

David's gaze moved from the record to her fingers.

"Of course."

She crossed to the console and hesitated.

He came to stand beside her.

"Do you know how?"

"Yes," she said. "I'm not twelve."

His mouth curved faintly. "I asked because you were holding your breath."

"I don't want to damage it."

"You won't."

"You sound confident."

"I am watching your hands."

Her fingers tightened on the edge of the sleeve.

Slowly, she looked at him.

David's gaze had indeed settled on her hands.

Not casually.

With the same disturbing focus he gave her face, her voice, the hollow at her throat.

Her pulse shifted.

His eyes flicked upward as if he heard it.

Ember pulled the record out before she lost her nerve and placed it on the turntable.

David stepped closer to adjust a small lever near her wrist.

This time, his fingers brushed her skin.

Cold.

A deliberate accident.

Or accidental deliberation.

She could no longer tell with him.

The needle lowered.

Static bloomed.

Then music filled the apartment.

The first notes unlocked something inside her so quickly she hated it. Ember had not heard the album in years, not since her mother's tiny apartment, not since open windows and wet brushes in jars, not since childhood Sundays before life taught everyone the price of staying soft.

For a moment, she forgot David stood beside her.

Her throat tightened.

The singer's voice entered, low and aching.

Ember folded her arms across herself.

"Bad memory?" David asked.

"No."

"Good?"

"Complicated."

He accepted that without pressing.

Which, in David's case, meant he pressed by remaining silent.

She exhaled through a faint laugh. "You do that on purpose, too."

"What?"

"Wait."

He looked down at her.

"I have time."

The words were simple.

Too simple.

They opened beneath her like a stairwell in the dark.

Ember turned toward the windows.

Rain washed the glass. Beyond it, the cemetery gleamed under gaslight, its crypts pale, and patient. The music moved through the room with candle-warm sorrow.

"My mother used to dance to this while pretending she wasn't sad," Ember said. "I thought it was glamorous when I was little. Later, I realized adults do strange things to survive."

David stood beside her without speaking.

No pity.

Thank God.

"She'd paint women in black dresses," Ember continued. "Women at windows. Women with knives. Women with flowers. Never happy women. Beautiful ones, though. Always beautiful."

"She taught you to draw."

"Not deliberately. I watched."

"And do you also now draw women at windows?"

The accuracy of it startled her.

She looked at him.

"How would you know that?"

His gaze did not move from hers.

"You have charcoal beneath the nail of your right index finger."

Ember glanced down.

A dark smudge hid there, half-mooned beneath the nail tip.

"Could be from anything."

"It is charcoal."

"You're sure?"

"Yes."

A faint shiver crossed her skin.

David saw it.

Of course.

"Do I frighten you?" he asked quietly.

The question came without warning.

Ember stared at him.

The music trembled between them.

"Yes," she said.

His expression did not change.

Only his attention sharpened.

"Enough to leave?"

She should have said yes.

She did not.

"No."

The silence after that was longer than it needed to be.

David moved first. He stepped around her and approached the record shelves, giving her space with such elegant control it felt more dangerous than crowding her would have.

"You said you wanted to know the song," he murmured. "Now you know."

Ember watched him skim his fingers over the shelves.

The gesture was careful. Reverent.

As if each record contained a pulse.

"Do you collect anything else?" she asked.

"Yes."

"What?"

His head turned slightly.

"Moments."

She rolled her eyes before she could stop herself. "That was almost unbearable."

"And yet you asked."

"I regret encouraging you."

"No, you don't."

She hated how true that was.

He selected a slim gray record sleeve from the lower shelf and carried it to her.

"This one," he said.

Ember took it from him.

The cover showed a dark stage, blurred lights, and a woman in a black dress standing alone before a microphone.

"I don't know this."

"No."

"Should I?"

"No."

"Are you going to be cryptic all night?"

"Not all night."

"Merciful."

His eyes warmed again.

"This was recorded live in 1979. Small venue. Terrible acoustics. Extraordinary performance."

Ember studied the cover. "You sound as if you were there."

"I was."

She looked up.

David went still.

Not abruptly.

Worse.

Smoothly.

Like a curtain pulled across a window.

"You were what?" she asked.

"There."

"In 1979."

"Yes."

"You would have been, what, negative ten?"

His expression remained unreadable.

"That would have been difficult."

"David."

The name came out more softly than she intended.

His eyes narrowed by the slightest degree, as if hearing it from her mouth affected him physically.

Interesting.

"You caught that," he said.

"I possess basic math skills."

"A devastating advantage."

"Do not charm your way out of this."

"I would never."

"You would absolutely."

A faint smile touched him.

Then faded.

Ember held the record between them.

"How old are you?"

A log shifted inside the unlit fireplace as if moved by a phantom hand.

No fire. No wind.

Still, something clicked softly in the room.

David's gaze remained on her face.

"Older than I appear."

"That is not an answer."

"No."

"Is it the only one I'm getting?"

"For now."

Her heartbeat had begun doing unreasonable things.

David glanced toward her throat again.

This time, he caught himself and looked away.

That made everything worse.

Because now she knew he could stop himself.

He had simply chosen not to before.

Ember set the record down on the console.

"Are all of your friends older than they appear?"

"Most."

"Are they dangerous?"

"Yes."

No hesitation.

She swallowed. "Are you?"

David stepped closer.

Not enough to crowd.

Enough to make retreat a question.

"Yes."

The word did not land like a threat.

It landed like a confession.

Ember moved her fingers to rest against the edge of the console. His hand settled on the polished wood beside hers, close enough that his pinky ring nearly touched her skin.

"Then why invite me here?" she asked.

His gaze lowered to the narrow space between their hands.

"Because danger does not interest me half as much as restraint."

Her mouth went dry.

"And I'm supposed to trust your restraint?"

"No."

His eyes lifted to hers.

"You are supposed to notice it."

The room changed around them.

Or maybe Ember did.

The record ended behind them, the needle catching softly in the inner groove.

Rhythmic static filled the silence.

A heartbeat made of dust.

David's hand remained beside hers.

He did not touch.

He did not move.

He let the not-touching gather weight until Ember's body understood it as plainly as contact.

"You listen with your whole body," he said softly.

She laughed once, but it came out uneven. "That sounds like an accusation."

"It was admiration."

"Do you ever admire things normally?"

"No."

"At least you're consistent."

"Only with worthy things."

Her fingers flexed.

The silver ring on his pinky brushed her knuckle.

This time, neither of them could pretend accident.

Static crackled.

Rain breathed against the windows.

David looked at their hands and drew in a slow breath through his nose, almost too subtle to catch.

Almost.

Then he removed his hand from the console.

Ember should have been relieved.

Instead, something in her mourned the lost inch.

"Another record?" he asked.

His voice had gone lower.

Careful.

Controlled.

She looked toward the shelves, then back at him.

It would be smart to leave.

It would be sane.

It would also mean returning across the hall to a quiet apartment and pretending this room had not rearranged several private pieces of her.

"One more," she said.

David's eyes darkened.

Only slightly.

Enough.

"One," he agreed.

But when he turned toward the shelves, Ember already knew he was lying.

Not because the word was false.

Because the ritual had begun.

YOU COME TO MY door because of the music.

That is what you will tell yourself.

I allow you the lie because it is elegant in its smallness.

You stand in my hallway barefoot, wrapped in black wool, pretending irritation hides curiosity. Your hair is loose tonight. Your mouth has no lipstick. There is charcoal beneath one fingernail and sleeplessness beneath your eyes.

I should not like you this way more.

I do.

When you cross my threshold, the apartment changes.

Not visibly.

The candles do not flare. The rain does not pause. The records remain where they have waited for years.

But I know.

The room has accepted you.

You move toward the shelves as if drawn by instinct. Careful hands. Curious eyes. No greed. No performance. You do not touch until you are invited.

Beautiful girl.

Do you know how rare restraint looks on the living?

You find your mother's record, and grief slips through you before you can close the door on it. I watch the memory strike. Your shoulders shift. Your mouth tightens. You fold yourself around the ache before it spills.

You think I want your beauty first.

I do.

I am not noble enough to pretend otherwise.

But beauty is common in rooms like mine. Beauty has sat on my furniture, drunk from my glasses, slept beneath my roof, begged for my mouth, my blood, my name.

You are not common.

You handle sorrow like a blade you learned to carry by the hilt.

That keeps me watching.

When you ask if I am dangerous, I tell you yes.

Not enough truth to satisfy you.

Enough to warn you.

Yet...

You stay.

Your hand rests beside mine on the console. Warm skin near cold metal. One inch between us. Less.

I could close it.

I could take your wrist and hear your pulse through my thumb. I could pull you close enough to learn whether you taste more like rain or old grief.

Instead, I do nothing.

And you notice.

Good.

Notice the space I leave.

Notice the hunger I do not spend.

Notice that restraint is not absence.

It is appetite taught manners.

You ask for one more record.

One.

As if either of us believes in endings tonight.

Chapter 6
White Roses

By Wednesday, Ember had stopped pretending David Caesarius was a temporary problem.

Temporary problems did not rearrange a person's evenings.

Temporary problems did not train her body to recognize the sound of vinyl through walls with humiliating precision.

And temporary problems certainly did not result in her standing in front of a flower cart in the French Quarter at dusk while arguing internally over whether white roses had become emotionally compromised.

"You're thinking too hard again," the florist informed her.

Ember looked up.

The old woman behind the cart sat wrapped in layers of black shawls despite the humid evening air. Silver rings covered nearly every finger. A cigarette burned slowly between two of them while misty fog floated softly over the narrow street.

"You can tell?" Ember asked.

"You've picked up and put down those roses four times."

"That's fair."

The florist narrowed her eyes toward the bouquet in Ember's hands.

"Funeral?"

"Sort of."

"Man trouble?"

Ember barked out a laugh before she could stop herself.

"Baby, you're in New Orleans holding white roses in the fog, wearing black lipstick." The woman responded to her laugh, gesturing vaguely with her cigarette. "Either somebody died or somebody dangerous looked at you too long."

Heat crawled immediately into Ember's face.

Interesting.

Concerning.

Annoying.

The florist smiled slowly.

"Ah," she murmured. "So, it's the second thing."

Ember paid for the flowers without answering.

The rain had softened by the time she returned to Marceaux House. Not a storm tonight. Just silver mist drifting over the cemetery gates and turning the gas lamps outside into blurred halos.

She climbed the stairs more slowly than usual; flowers wrapped carefully in brown paper against her chest.

The hallway on the fourth floor stood empty.

David's door remained closed.

No music.

No light beneath the frame.

A ridiculous thread of disappointment tugged through her before she could stop it.

Ember unlocked her apartment and stepped inside.

Darkness greeted her.

Not unsettling darkness.

Waiting darkness.

The kind old buildings wore naturally.

She crossed toward the bay windows switching on a lamp near the bookshelf. Warm amber light spilled slowly through the apartment.

Misty fog moved softly beyond the glass.

The cemetery below gleamed pale and wet beneath the evening sky.

Ember loosened her coat and approached the windows automatically.

The Grant crypt stood beneath the magnolia tree, marble slick with moisture. White flowers from earlier visits rested against the iron gate in ghost-pale clusters.

Her great-grandfather had purchased permanence beautifully.

She wondered if he had known what a strange gift survival could become.

A soft knock sounded.

Not at the apartment door.

At the bay window.

Ember startled hard enough to nearly drop the flowers still in her hands.

David stood on the narrow connecting balcony outside the glass.

Of course he did.

Mist silvered his dark hair. Black coat damp at the shoulders. One hand tucked into his pocket while the other rested lightly against the window frame.

Beautiful men should not be allowed to materialize outside windows on foggy nights.

It encouraged poor decisions.

Ember crossed the room and unlocked the latch of the glass door to her portion of the narrow iron balcony.

The instant she pushed it open, cool air flooded the apartment, carrying wet stone, night-blooming flowers, cigarette smoke, and David.

"You use doors strangely," she informed him.

"I use them when necessary."

"That sounds like something a supernatural entity says before haunting someone."

His gaze lowered briefly to the roses in her hands.

"You bought more."

The words softened slightly.

Not enough for most people to notice.

Enough for her.

Ember stepped aside to let him enter from the balcony.

David moved with the same quiet precision he carried everywhere else. Water glimmered briefly along the shoulders of his black coat before he removed it smoothly and draped it across the back of a chair.

He looked around her apartment once.

Not critically.

Attentively.

The lamp.

The unpacked books.

The charcoal sketches scattered across the dining table.

The roses.

"You've changed things," he observed.

"I live here."

"Yes."

That single word carried strange weight from him.

As though the fact pleased him more than it should.

Ember crossed toward the kitchen sink and unwrapped the flowers carefully.

"You disappeared," she said casually.

David leaned one shoulder against the archway separating the kitchen from the living room.

"Did I?"

"You know you did."

"I had business."

"You sound like a Victorian widower."

"I will take that as a compliment."

"You shouldn't."

His eyes followed her hands as she trimmed the stems beneath running water.

There it was again.

That attention.

That unbearable, focused observation.

"You always cut them diagonally," he murmured.

Ember glanced toward him.

"What?"

"The stems." His gaze dipped toward the sink. "You cut them diagonally to help them absorb water."

A pause.

"You've done it every time."

Something low and warm unfurled in her stomach.

Not because he noticed.

Because he remembered.

"You study people like research," she said softly.

"No."

David's voice lowered slightly.

"Only you."

The room quieted around the words.

Rain ticked softly against the windows.

Ember arranged the flowers into an old glass vase she'd found in one of the kitchen cabinets two days earlier.

"You really don't know how to flirt normally, do you?"

"I have never seen the appeal in pretending interest casually."

"That sounds exhausting."

"It is efficient."

She laughed softly despite herself.

David watched the sound happen to her mouth.

Actually, watched it.

Ember became abruptly aware of the apartment around them: the dim lights, the rain outside, the flowers, the narrowness of the room with him inside it.

Private gravity.

That was the phrase for this now.

Somehow, impossibly, they had developed private gravity.

"What was your business?" she asked, carrying the vase toward the bay windows.

David followed slowly.

"Adrien required assistance."

"That sounds ominous."

"It usually is."

"Should I ask for details?"

"No."

"Good. I wasn't going to."

The corner of his mouth shifted faintly.

Ember set the flowers on a small table near the windowsill, where lamplight brushed the pale petals gold.

Outside, mist drifted across the cemetery paths.

David stopped beside her.

Close.

Not touching.

Never touching first anymore.

As if he had learned exactly how dangerous restraint became between them.

"You missed the music," he said quietly.

Ember looked toward him sharply.

His gaze remained on the cemetery below.

Not teasing.

Not smug.

Observing.

Truth again.

"You noticed that too?" she asked.

"Yes."

"Of course you did."

"You stood outside my door Sunday night for forty-three seconds before I opened it."

Her breath caught.

David turned his head slightly.

Rain-shadowed eyes met hers.

"You count?" she asked softly.

"I notice."

The correction entered her bloodstream like heat.

Forty-three seconds.

Not approximately.

Not maybe.

Exactly.

God.

"You make it very difficult to decide whether this is romantic or deeply alarming."

"I imagine it can be both."

The answer should not have made her pulse jump.

It did.

Below them, lightning flickered faintly behind distant clouds. The cemetery glowed white for one brief heartbeat before darkness reclaimed it.

Ember folded her arms loosely against the chill drifting through the open balcony door.

"I used to think cemeteries were frightening," she admitted quietly.

"And now?"

"Now I think they're honest."

David looked at her then.

Fully.

The intensity of it nearly stole the next breath from her lungs.

"Explain."

The word came softly.

Interested.

Ember stared out toward the crypts again before answering.

"When you're in New York long enough, everything becomes a performance." She shrugged lightly. "Money. Careers. Relationships. Everybody trying to look untouched by exhaustion."

David listened silently.

"The cemetery doesn't do that," she continued. "It's honest about what people are. Temporary. Grieving. Loved. Forgotten." Her fingers brushed lightly against the vase. "There's something peaceful about that."

Rain whispered harder against the glass.

For a moment, David said nothing.

Then:

"You speak to him sometimes."

Ember looked toward him slowly.

"Your great-grandfather."

Not a question.

Again, he had noticed.

"Yes," she admitted quietly.

"You lower your voice when you do."

The intimacy of the observation made her chest tighten unexpectedly.

"I didn't realize anyone could hear."

"I hear many things."

His gaze moved toward the cemetery below.

"You thank him."

"How do you know that?"

"You smile afterward."

The room seemed to tilt slightly around her.

No one had ever observed her this carefully before.

Not lovers.

Not friends.

Not family.

David noticed things the way storms noticed coastlines.

Thoroughly.

Inevitably.

"Why?" she asked softly.

His eyes returned to hers.

"Why, what?"

"Why pay this much attention to me?"

The question settled heavily between them.

Rain.

Candles.

White roses.

David standing close enough that cold drifted subtly from his skin into the warmth of the room.

He could have lied.

Could have flirted.

Deflected.

Smiled his elegant, almost-smile and escaped sideways.

Instead, he answered her honestly.

"Because I want to."

The words entered her body like dark wine.

No performance.

No seduction layered over them.

Only truth.

And somehow that truth felt infinitely more dangerous.

Ember's throat tightened.

David's eyes dropped there instantly.

A pause entered him.

Sharp.

Controlled.

Then, slowly, he lifted one hand.

Not toward her face.

Toward her hair.

Ember went completely still.

Rain breathed softly through the cracked door.

David's fingers brushed a strand of damp auburn hair from her shoulder with unbearable care.

Cold fingertips against warm skin.

The contact lasted barely seconds.

Long enough.

His knuckles grazed the side of her throat before his hand fell away again.

Ember forgot how breathing worked.

David seemed affected too.

His gaze lingered on the place he had touched with dangerous stillness.

Not hunger exactly.

Worse.

Restraint fighting hunger.

The room thickened around them.

Neither moved.

Neither spoke.

Then, softly:

"You should sleep, Ember."

Her pulse stumbled again.

Not because of the words.

Because of the way he said her name.

Like something he already possessed privately.

Ember swallowed once. "That sounded less like concern and more like a command."

A faint shadow crossed his mouth.

"Perhaps."

"David."

His eyes lifted to hers immediately.

She hated how responsive he became to his name from her mouth.

"What happens," she asked carefully, "if I stop being interesting to you?"

Silence.

Outside, thunder rolled softly across the city.

David studied her face for one long, measured moment.

Then stepped closer.

Enough that cold wrapped gently around her warmth.

Enough that she could smell rain in his hair.

"You will not," he said quietly.

The certainty in his voice terrified her.

Because she believed him.

And judging by the darkness moving beneath David's eyes as he looked at her beside the white roses and cemetery rain...

So did he.

You buy white roses again.

By now, the florist recognizes the shape of your rituals. The old women of this city always do. New Orleans notices repetition the way old predators notice blood in water.

You carry the flowers against your chest while rain gathers silver in your hair.

I watch from the balcony.

Of course I do.

You no longer startle when you sense me nearby. Your body still reacts. Your pulse still changes. But some private instinct inside you has stopped treating my attention as intrusion.

Good.

That instinct is learning.

When you open the balcony door for me, warm apartment air folds around rain and night. Your rooms smell like charcoal, coffee grounds, old paper, and the roses in your hands.

You are beginning to leave yourself inside this place.

I approve.

You trim the stems beneath running water while I watch your fingers work carefully through the ritual. Diagonal cuts. Fresh water. Arrangement before placement.

Tender things reveal themselves through habits.

You think I study you because I am fascinated.

I do.

But fascination is only the beginning of attention.

I study you because every night I leave your apartment knowing more than I did before.

How your breathing changes when you lie.

How your mouth curves before genuine laughter.

How loneliness sharpened you without hardening you completely.

How you touch flowers as though bruising them would feel personal.

You ask why I pay attention to you.

Because I want to.

Such a small answer for such a dangerous truth.

The actual answer would frighten you.

Not because I want your body.

I do.

That remains the simplest part of this.

No.

The danger is that I have begun organizing my nights around your existence.

The records begin because you might hear them.

The door remains unlocked because you might come.

The hours shape themselves around the possibility of your footsteps in the hallway.

You ask what happens if you stop being interesting.

Beautiful girl.

You still believe attention behaves rationally.

When I touch your hair, your pulse stumbles hard enough that I feel it in my teeth.

And for one disastrous moment, I imagine pressing my mouth against your throat beside the white roses while rain buries the city outside.

Instead, I step back.

Instead, I tell you to sleep.

Instead, I leave with my restraint intact.

But the wanting follows me across the hall like a second shadow.

And tonight, for the first time in many years, I understand something profoundly inconvenient.

I am beginning to crave your presence more than your blood.

Chapter 7

The Shape of Attention

By Friday night, Ember knew the rhythms of David Caesarius with humiliating precision.

Not facts.

Rhythms.

Facts were simple things:

He preferred vinyl to digital music

He drank red wine almost exclusively

He smoked only on the balcony

He wore black with the devotion of a man   who had made mourning aesthetic

Rhythms were worse.

Rhythms meant she knew:

which floorboards inside his apartment   creaked before he opened the door

how long he usually let silence sit before   answering a question

when his music shifted from jazz into   darker, slower things after midnight

the exact cadence of his footsteps   crossing the hall

Rhythms meant her body noticed his absence before her mind admitted it.

And tonight, he was absent.

Ember stood at her bay window, watching rain collect along the cemetery paths while unease crawled beneath her ribs.

No music.

No faint glow beneath his door.

Nothing.

The silence across the hall felt wrong now.

That realization alone should have alarmed her more than it did.

She lifted her wineglass and stared down into the cemetery below.

Friday again.

One week since the poetry reading.

One week since David had looked at her across candlelight and recited obsession like confession.

The city beyond Marceaux House breathed softly beneath rain and fog. Somewhere farther down the avenue, jazz drifted faintly through the mist.

Ember should sketch.

Read.

Sleep.

Call someone from New York.

Rejoin normal society.

Instead, she stood at the window, listening to the absence of a man she had known for less than two weeks.

Pathetic.

The worst part?

She missed him.

Not abstractly.

Physically.

The apartment itself seemed aware of it.

Her rooms felt too still tonight. The candles burned lower. The cemetery beyond the windows looked colder somehow without vinyl threading softly through the walls.

Private gravity.

God.

She hated that phrase now.

A sharp knock interrupted the thought.

Ember turned too quickly, wine sloshing dangerously inside the glass.

Three knocks this time.

At the front door.

Not the balcony.

Interesting.

She crossed the apartment and opened the door without checking first.

Sabine Ortiz, her neighbor from the second floor, stood in the hallway, holding a cigarette in one hand and a paper grocery sack in the other.

"Well," Sabine drawled immediately. "You look disappointed."

Ember blinked. "Excuse me?"

"That I'm not your vampire."

Heat climbed instantly into her face.

Sabine smiled around the cigarette.

The woman looked magnificent tonight in a black silk shirt layered over dark jeans and heavy silver jewelry. Her dramatic eyeliner had smudged slightly at the corners, giving her the appearance of a woman who either knew too much or intended to.

Possibly both.

"I don't have a vampire," Ember informed her.

"Mhm."

"I don't."

Sabine held up the grocery sack. "Your packages got dropped downstairs again. I rescued them from the lobby before the building swallowed them whole."

"Oh," Ember exhaled. "Thank you."

"You're welcome."

Sabine handed over the bag but made no move to leave.

Instead, her eyes drifted once toward David's dark apartment door across the hall.

"No music tonight," she observed casually.

Ember hated how quickly she answered.

"No."

Sabine's mouth twitched.

"You've started listening for it."

"That sounds creepier when you say it aloud."

"Most truths do."

The older woman leaned one shoulder against the hallway wall and studied Ember carefully.

"Let me give you some neighborly advice."

"Oh good. Those words never end badly."

"Do not let the beautiful people in this building convince you they're harmless."

Ember's fingers tightened slightly around the grocery bag.

"Has David hurt someone?"

Sabine looked genuinely amused.

"Honey, that's not the question you should be asking."

A small chill moved beneath Ember's skin.

Before she could respond, footsteps sounded on the staircase below.

Slow.

Measured.

Familiar.

Her pulse reacted instantly.

Sabine noticed that too.

"Ah," she murmured softly. "There he is."

David appeared at the top of the stairs moments later, black coat damp from rain, dark hair touched silver beneath the hallway sconces.

His eyes found Ember immediately.

Not Sabine.

Ember.

The intensity of his focus hit her physically now. Like warmth. Like pressure. Like something invisible settling carefully against her skin.

Then his gaze shifted toward Sabine.

"Sabine."

"David."

The temperature in the hallway changed subtly.

Not hostility.

Recognition sharpened into caution.

Sabine walked over and flicked ash neatly into a crystal tray balanced on the hall windowsill.

"Your girl looked lonely," she informed him.

David's eyes returned to Ember at once.

Something moved behind them.

Fast.

Dark.

Possessive enough to tighten the air.

Ember felt it immediately.

So did Sabine.

Interesting.

"She is not my girl," David said calmly.

Sabine arched one eyebrow. “That’s what we’re pretending tonight?”

“Sabine,” Ember warned weakly.

The older woman laughed softly.

Then, mercifully, she pushed away from the wall.

“Relax, querida. If he wanted you dead, he’d look much happier.”

And with that deeply concerning statement, she disappeared toward the stairs, trailing smoke and silver jewelry.

Silence settled across the hallway.

Rain whispered faintly beyond the cemetery windows.

David looked at Ember.

Fully.

Directly.

Dangerously.

“You opened the door without checking first,” he said quietly.

Not a greeting.

Not hello.

That.

Ember blinked. “Good evening to you too.”

“You should be more careful.”

“You sound annoyed.”

“I am.”

The words landed harder than they should have.

Because beneath the irritation lived something else.

Relief.

David crossed the hallway toward her slowly.

His coat carried rain and cold air into the warm corridor.

“You disappeared tonight,” Ember said before she could stop herself.

The moment the words escaped, she regretted them.

Not because they were inaccurate.

Because they were revealing.

David stopped directly in front of her.

Close enough now that she could smell wet wool, clove smoke, and rainwater cooling against dark fabric.

“I had business,” he said softly.

“You used that excuse already.”

“And you disliked it the first time.”

“You noticed that too?”

"Yes."

Of course.

His gaze moved over her face carefully.

Cataloguing.

Absorbing.

The hallway suddenly felt much narrower than before.

"You missed the music tonight," he observed.

There it was again.

Truth offered without embarrassment.

Ember looked away first, toward the cemetery windows at the end of the hall.

"Yes," she admitted quietly.

The silence after that shifted something fundamental between them.

Because now he knew.

Not suspected.

Not hoped.

Knew.

David's breathing changed slightly.

Barely perceptible.

But Ember had begun learning his rhythms too.

Interesting.

Dangerous.

His eyes lowered briefly to the wineglass still in her hand.

Then to her mouth.

Then back to her eyes.

"I missed you as well," he said.

The hallway vanished.

Not physically.

But the world narrowed abruptly around those words.

No flirtation.

No smoothness.

No practiced seduction.

Only truth spoken quietly enough to ruin her pulse completely.

Ember stared at him.

Rain moved softly beyond the windows.

David held her gaze with terrifying steadiness.

And suddenly she understood something she had been carefully avoiding for days now.

This was no longer curiosity.

No longer fascination.

She had started arranging parts of herself around him, too.

The realization hit like stepping through rotten floorboards into deep water.

"You say things," she murmured faintly, "that should not work as well as they do."

"I rarely say things I do not mean."

"That's somehow worse."

"Yes."

His gaze lingered on her mouth another dangerous second.

Then shifted toward her apartment behind her.

"Were you going somewhere?"

"No."

"Good."

The word settled low inside her.

God.

David reached up slowly.

Ember went still instinctively.

His fingers brushed lightly against the sleeve of her sweater near the wrist.

A tiny movement.

Barely contact.

Yet her body reacted instantly.

His eyes darkened.

"There's charcoal here," he murmured.

Ember glanced down.

A faint black smudge streaked the cuff.

"I was sketching."

"What?"

"Nothing useful."

"I doubt that."

The attention in his voice moved through her like heat under skin.

David's fingertips remained against her sleeve one moment too long.

Then he withdrew them carefully.

Restraint again.

Always restraint.

Ember was beginning to understand how deliberate it was.

How difficult it might actually be.

"How was your business?" she asked softly.

David's expression shifted almost imperceptibly.

Cooler.

"Unpleasant."

"Adrien-related unpleasant or murder-related unpleasant?"

One corner of his mouth moved faintly.

"Those categories overlap more often than they should."

"That is an insane sentence."

"It is an accurate one."

She laughed despite herself.

David watched the laugh happen again.

Not the joke.

Her.

Always her.

"You're tired," he observed quietly.

"I didn't sleep well."

His gaze sharpened.

"Why?"

The question came too quickly.

Too intensely.

Ember hesitated.

Because the actual answer was: the apartment felt wrong without you in it somewhere.

Absolutely not.

Instead, she shrugged lightly.

"Too much coffee."

David looked unconvinced.

Good.

He should suffer slightly, too.

A faint smile touched Ember's mouth at the thought.

David noticed immediately.

"What?"

"Nothing."

"Ember."

The low warning threaded through her name nearly dissolved her spine.

She swallowed once.

Dangerous man.

"Maybe," she admitted carefully, "the building has become quieter lately."

Understanding entered his face slowly.

Not surprise.

Recognition.

The hallway seemed to tighten around both of them.

"I see," he said softly.

"No, you don't."

"I do."

"You're smug now."

"Only internally."

"That still counts."

"Yes."

Rain struck the windows harder suddenly.

Lightning flashed pale across the cemetery-facing glass.

For one suspended instant, David stood illuminated silver-white in the corridor.

Dark coat.

Pale throat.

Watchful eyes.

Water still clinging to his hair.

Beautiful enough to ruin people.

Ember's chest tightened unexpectedly.

Because she had missed this.

His voice.

His presence.

The shape of him standing near her door, like he belonged there.

Which perhaps he did now.

Or worse: perhaps she wanted him to.

David looked at her for one long, measured moment.

Then quietly:

"Come across the hall."

Her pulse jumped instantly.

"You make that sound suspicious."

"It is."

"That honesty again."

"I thought we established you preferred it."

She did.

That was the problem.

Ember glanced once toward her apartment behind her.

Warm lights.

Half-finished sketchbook.

Solitude.

Then toward David.

Rain-darkened black wool.

Cold fingertips.

Vinyl waiting somewhere behind his door.

Eyes that studied her like she was becoming necessary.

The choice barely qualified as one.

"You're impossible," she muttered.

David's gaze lowered briefly toward her mouth again.

"Yes."

And God help her, she followed him anyway.

YOU MISS ME.

The realization enters you reluctantly.

Beautifully.

You stand at your window, pretending the silence across the hall does not affect you while your body listens for records that never begin.

The apartment notices before you do.

Rooms understand absence instinctively.

Especially rooms that have begun expecting another person inside them.

Sabine smells it on you immediately.

Her kind has always been irritatingly perceptive.

When I reach the fourth floor and find her outside your door, your pulse changes before you even turn toward me.

Relief.

Such a lovely sound inside the body.

You ask where I was.

Not casually enough.

Good.

You are beginning to reveal yourself accidentally.

That is where honesty becomes most dangerous.

When you admit missing the music, I feel the words like fingertips beneath my skin.

You have grown accustomed to me.

My voice.

My records.

My presence in the hallway after midnight.

The shape of attention has changed.

At first, you merely endured being watched.

Now you search for the watcher.

Do you understand what that means?

Not yet.

But your body does.

Your pulse steadies when I stand near you. Your breathing slows when I speak. The building itself has begun teaching you my rhythms.

And tonight, when I touch the charcoal on your sleeve, your entire nervous system answers before your mouth does.

Beautiful girl.

You are learning me by instinct now.

That is when fascination becomes irreversible.

I tell you to come across the hall because I need to hear your footsteps follow me.

Need is an ugly word.

I have avoided it for a very long time.

Yet, there it is.

Waiting beneath my ribs each night, you remain near me.

And when you step forward to follow me once again, I understand something with devastating clarity.

I no longer crave merely possessing your attention.

I crave being expected by you.

Chapter 8

The Second Salon

The next invitation did not arrive in an envelope.

It waited on Ember's threshold at sunset the following Friday in the form of a single white rose tied with black silk ribbon.

No card.

No wax seal.

No calligraphy.

Only the flower lying against the dark wood floor, as if placed there by someone with an intimate understanding of precision.

Ember stood in the hallway for a long moment, staring down at it.

The fourth floor of Marceaux House remained quiet around her. Rain freckled the arched window at the far end of the corridor. The old sconces trembled with amber light. Across the hall, David's black door remained closed.

Of course.

He would not knock.

He had moved beyond knocking days ago.

Ember crouched and picked up the rose.

The stem had been stripped of thorns. Every petal remained intact, pale and cool against her fingertips. The black ribbon was tied in a neat knot, almost severe, save for the faint scent clinging to the silk.

Clove smoke.

Wine.

Rain.

David.

Heat unfurled low in her stomach before she could stop it.

"Ridiculous," she whispered.

The rose offered no argument.

Inside her apartment, the rooms were already glowing with early evening blue. Fog pressed softly against the cemetery windows, softening the marble crypts into pale shapes beneath the magnolia branches. Ember placed the rose on her dressing table and stood before her mirror.

She knew what it meant.

Another salon.

Another gathering.

Another evening of candlelight, wine, old poetry, beautiful people with too-still smiles, and David Caesarius watching her as though she had become the final line of a prayer he had no intention of sharing.

She should choose something casual.

Something unrevealing.

Something practical enough to prove she had not dressed for him.

Instead, she chose a black satin dress she had not worn in two years.

It had thin straps, a low back, and a slit that ran high enough along one thigh to make morality feel hypothetical. The neckline draped softly without exposing too much, which somehow felt worse. Silver earrings brushed her jaw when she moved. Her dark auburn hair fell loose, intentionally wild, and she painted her mouth the color of bruised cherries.

She stared at herself.

"You are not dressing for him," she informed her reflection.

Her reflection, traitorous thing, looked unconvinced.

At eight o'clock, music slipped beneath David's door.

Not piano this time.

Cello first.

Low.

Slow.

Then a violin joined, thin and aching, threading itself through the hall like a blade wrapped in velvet.

Ember took the white rose from her dressing table and crossed the corridor.

David's door opened before she reached it.

He stood there.

Waiting.

Black shirt.

Black trousers.

No coat.

Silver rings.

Dark hair brushed back from his face, except for one loose strand at his temple.

His gaze dropped to the rose in her hand.

Then lifted.

And stopped.

Whatever greeting he had prepared died before it reached his mouth.

Ember felt the silence like fingers sliding down her spine.

His eyes moved over her with terrifying care. The dress. Her bare shoulders. The dark shine of her mouth. The line of her throat. The slit against her thigh where black satin parted around skin.

No smile touched him.

No compliment came.

That, somehow, was worse.

Because his stillness changed.

It tightened.

His fingers curled once around the doorframe before easing open again.

A tiny movement.

Almost nothing.

Ember saw it.

Good.

Let him suffer.

"You left a rose," she said.

His eyes returned to hers.

"Yes."

"No invitation?"

"You know you're invited."

The words struck lower than they should have.

Behind him, the apartment glowed with candles and voices. Laughter moved through the room, low and elegant. Wineglass crystal touched wood. Rain hissed softly against the cemetery windows.

Ember lifted the rose slightly. "Was I supposed to understand this?"

"You did."

"Arrogant."

"Accurate."

She stepped closer.

David did not move back.

For one suspended moment, they stood at his threshold with the old hallway behind her and candlelit warmth behind him.

His gaze lowered to her mouth.

"Ember," he said quietly.

It sounded less like her name and more like restraint wearing thin.

"Yes?"

A faint muscle worked in his jaw.

Then he stepped aside.

"Come in."

The apartment was full again.

But different now.

That was the first thing Ember noticed.

The same velvet furniture. Same towering bookshelves. Same dark wallpaper and black candles. Same rain pressing silver trails down the bay windows overlooking the cemetery.

The same guests, mostly.

Adrien Avenoire lounged near the fireplace in immaculate black, one pale hand resting against the back of Thessa Rigby's chair. Thessa wore wine-red velvet tonight, her rosary wrapped twice around one wrist, her eyes sharp as she watched Ember enter.

Lucien Roptera stood beside the record player with a glass of red wine and a faintly concerned expression he disguised poorly.

There were others too, faces Ember vaguely remembered from the first salon.

But this time, when they turned toward her, the room shifted differently.

Not curiosity.

Recognition.

As if a fact had clarified since the last time.

As if she had crossed the hall often enough to be measured, discussed, and perhaps quietly catalogued.

Adrien's mouth curved.

"Ember Grant," he said, voice smooth as poison poured over ice. "There she is."

David's attention sharpened instantly behind her.

Ember felt it before she saw anyone react to it.

His presence at her back became … denser.

Adrien's smile widened.

"Careful," Thessa murmured without looking at him. "You're enjoying yourself too soon."

"I usually do."

Lucien crossed toward Ember before Adrien could say more.

"Wine?" he offered.

"Please."

His gaze moved briefly over her face, then to David behind her.

A private warning passed through Lucien's expression.

Not to her.

To David.

Interesting.

David ignored it completely.

Lucien handed Ember a glass and lowered his voice. "You look lovely tonight."

"Thank you."

"Dangerously so."

That startled a laugh from her. "Is that a compliment or a safety advisory?"

"In this room?" Lucien glanced toward Adrien. "Both."

Adrien lifted his glass from across the room. "We can hear you."

Lucien did not look away from Ember. "I know."

The exchange should have amused her.

Instead, Ember became aware of how everyone seemed to be watching David by not watching him.

Like one watched a storm gather over water.

She turned.

David stood near the door, still as marble, his eyes fixed on Lucien's hand where it had briefly touched her elbow while handing over the wine.

Lucien noticed too.

His expression shifted.

Softly.

Warning again.

"David," Lucien said.

Only his name.

Nothing more.

David's gaze lifted from Ember's elbow to Lucien's face.

The room cooled.

Not literally.

But emotionally, instantly.

Conversation faltered at the edges. One of the women near the bookshelf stopped mid-sentence. Thessa's fingers paused against her glass. Adrien's smile became sharper, delighted and unwise.

Then David blinked once.

The room breathed again.

He crossed to Ember and stood beside her, close enough that his sleeve brushed hers.

Not possessive.

Not openly.

Not quite.

"You have wine?" he asked.

Ember glanced up at him.

"Yes."

"Good."

That was all.

But something in the guests' attention changed.

As though he had touched her much more intimately than he had.

Adrien laughed softly into his glass.

"Oh, this is exquisite."

David's eyes did not leave Ember. "Behave."

"Never."

Thessa finally looked at Ember fully. Her gaze moved with frank fascination over the rose in Ember's hand, the dress, the closeness of David at her side.

"So," Thessa said, voice warm and low. "You came back."

Ember lifted her glass. "Despite better judgment."

"All worthwhile things happen despite better judgment."

Adrien leaned toward Thessa with theatrical affection. "Darling, you say such romantic little disasters."

"You mistake memory for romance."

His smile sharpened.

David's fingers brushed the inside of Ember's wrist.

Light.

Quick.

Hidden from most of the room by the angle of their bodies.

But Ember felt it like a struck match.

Her breath caught before she could stop it.

David looked down at her.

Not at his hand.

At her face.

Watching the reaction.

Always watching.

"You're staring again," she murmured.

"Yes."

"Guests."

"I noticed."

"That usually implies social restraint."

His gaze lowered to her mouth.

"I am exercising restraint."

The words moved through her bloodstream with wicked heat.

Across the room, Adrien made a soft, delighted sound.

Lucien said, "Adrien."

"What? I said nothing."

"Your expression spoke."

"My expression is innocent."

"Your expression has never been innocent."

Ember almost laughed.

Then someone she did not know approached.

He was younger-looking than the others, with dark curls, warm brown skin, and a narrow gold hoop in one ear. Handsome in a softer way than David, with a smile meant to reassure rather than unsettle.

"Forgive me," he said to Ember. "I don't believe we've been introduced. Mateo Sable."

Ember accepted his offered hand.

"Ember Grant."

His fingers were warm.

Human warm.

A strange thing to notice.

His smile deepened. “I know. David’s poem last week was difficult to misinterpret.”

Heat climbed into Ember’s cheeks.

David went utterly still beside her.

Mateo’s gaze flicked briefly to him and back to Ember, either brave or foolish enough to continue. “I wondered whether anyone could live up to that much attention.”

“And?” Ember asked, because apparently curiosity had survived all her recent bad choices.

Mateo’s eyes traveled over her face.

Not rudely.

Appreciatively.

“I think he understated the matter.”

A sound entered the room.

Not loud.

Small.

Sharp.

Crystal fracturing beneath pressure.

Every head turned.

David still held his wineglass.

But a hairline crack had appeared along the bowl where his fingers curved around it.

Red wine bled through the fissure in a single dark line.

No one spoke.

The violin continued playing.

Rain tapped the windows.

Mateo’s smile vanished.

Ember looked at David.

His expression had not changed much.

That was the terrifying part.

No snarl.

No glare.

No visible rage.

Only quiet.

Absolute quiet.

The kind that emptied a room before anyone understood they were fleeing.

His eyes rested on Mateo with a stillness so precise it felt inhuman.

"Mateo," David said softly.

One word.

Mateo withdrew his hand from Ember's.

Slowly.

"Yes?"

"You are bleeding on my patience."

The sentence landed with awful elegance.

Mateo's face paled by a shade.

Adrien laughed once, low and delighted.

Thessa closed her eyes briefly. "Idiot man."

Lucien set his glass down with care. "David."

Again, only the name.

A warning.

David did not look at him.

The cracked wineglass remained in his hand, red sliding over his fingers like blood.

Ember's pulse pounded hard against her throat.

David's eyes flicked there.

Instantly.

And there it was.

For one fraction of a second, she saw something beneath him.

Not anger.

Not jealousy.

Hunger.

Focused.

Dark.

Ancient.

Her body answered with heat before fear could reach her.

David's nostrils flared almost imperceptibly.

He heard it.

Felt it.

Knew.

The room went painfully still.

Then Ember did the only thing she could think to do.

She reached for his glass.

"David."

His gaze snapped to hers.

The predator vanished behind his eyes.

Not gone.

Contained.

Barely.

Wine continued to spill over his fingers.

"You're making a mess," she said softly.

It was absurd.

Human.

Small enough to cross the terrible distance his silence had created.

David looked down at his hand as if noticing the glass for the first time.

Then back at her.

The corner of his mouth moved.

Not a smile.

Something darker.

"So I am."

He released the glass into her hand.

Carefully.

Obediently, almost.

A ripple moved through the room.

Thessa stared at Ember as if she had just done something astonishing.

Adrien's expression shifted from amusement to something sharper.

Interest.

Lucien exhaled very slowly.

Ember carried the cracked glass to the kitchen sink and set it down.

Her hands did not shake until after she released it.

David noticed.

Of course he did.

He crossed to her side before she could decide whether to be embarrassed.

His voice lowered for her alone.

"Did I frighten you?"

Yes.

No.

Not enough.

She looked up at him.

"A little."

His face tightened.

"Enough to leave?"

The question echoed Sunday night.

The answer came easier this time.

"No."

His eyes darkened.

Behind them, Adrien raised his glass.

"Well," he murmured. "To attention."

David did not look away from Ember.

"No," he said softly.

The room quieted again.

"To restraint."

No one laughed.

Not this time.

THE POETRY BEGAN LATER, though Ember could not say how much later.

Time had gone strange after the glass cracked.

The salon rearranged itself around the incident without openly acknowledging it. Mateo did not approach her again. Lucien watched David with an expression caught between concern and resignation. Thessa drew Ember briefly into conversation about art, hands, and whether every woman in New Orleans eventually learned to love cemetery flowers.

Adrien behaved beautifully.

Which was far more suspicious than his misbehavior.

And David stayed near Ember.

Never touching for long.

Never obviously claiming territory.

But always close enough that anyone entering their orbit would have to notice him.

His presence beside her had become less a position than a statement.

The poetry tonight carried a distinct flavor.

Last time had been fascination.

Tonight's salon, hunger.

Not crude hunger.

Not open wanting.

The hunger behind locked doors.

Inside mouths kept closed.

Of hands restrained by a strip of silk.

Thessa read first, her voice low and honeyed over the candlelit room.

A poem about a girl who fed wolves through iron bars and wondered why they remembered her name.

Then Lucien followed with something older, something in a language Ember did not know but understood anyway through the rhythm of it. It sounded like pleading before an altar. Like devotion resisting its own ruin.

Adrien, predictably, read something obscene enough to make Thessa sigh and Lucien remove his glasses.

Then David rose.

No one joked this time.

The silence formed around him instantly.

Ember sat near the bay window again, the cemetery silver behind her, the white rose resting in her lap.

David did not stand near the fireplace.

He stood before her.

Not close.

Not far.

Aligned so the entire room could see both of them.

Her mouth went dry.

He held no book.

No paper.

Only her gaze.

His voice began quietly.

"There are hungers that arrive with teeth
and hungers that arrive with manners.

The first announces itself honestly.
The second learns your door,
Your window,
Your favorite hour for looking at the rain."

Ember forgot to breathe.

David's eyes did not leave hers.

"I have known want crude enough to spend itself quickly.
Blood.
Beauty.
The brief mercy of forgetting one century inside another.
But this..."

His voice deepened slightly.

"This waits.
This stands in the hall and hears you move behind a locked door.
This knows the sound of your glass touching the windowsill.
This remembers white roses, charcoal fingers,
and the way your pulse changes
when you pretend not to be afraid."

The candlelight trembled.

Or maybe Ember did.

No one else existed now.

Not really.

The room had become a witness again.

"This is not hunger as appetite.
Appetite is easy.
Appetite takes.
This is hunger as devotion
and devotion as the last civilized form of possession."

A slow silence moved through the room.

David's gaze lowered briefly to her throat.

Then returned to her eyes.

"So let the saints keep their mercy.
Let the dead keep their flowers.
Let the windows keep their rain.
I will keep my hands open
until you step into them.
And when you do..."

His voice softened into something almost intimate enough to be indecent.

"I will not call it taking."

A pause.

His eyes burned dark.

"I will call it being answered."

The room remained silent when he finished.

Not reverent now.

Charged.

As if every candle had begun burning from both ends.

Ember could feel the poem under her skin.

In her throat.

Behind her knees.

At the center of every private place his attention had learned to find without touching.

Adrien looked delighted.

Thessa looked wary.

Lucien looked troubled.

David looked at Ember.

Only Ember.

The message had not been hidden this time.

It had been placed at her feet like the rose.

Offered.

Waiting.

Guests began leaving before midnight.

No one said why.

Mateo left first, which seemed wise.

Then the quieter couples. Then Lucien, who paused beside David near the door and spoke too softly for Ember to hear. David listened without expression.

Lucien glanced once toward Ember.

Concern again.

Then he left.

Adrien and Thessa were last.

Adrien kissed Ember's hand with theatrical slowness while watching David from beneath pale lashes.

"Survive the night, Miss Grant," he murmured.

Thessa pulled him toward the door before David could respond.

"Enough."

Adrien smiled over his shoulder.

"Never."

Then the door closed.

The apartment fell silent.

No guests.

No laughter.

No witnesses.

Only rain, candles, vinyl static, and David standing across the room looking at Ember as if the poem had not ended at all.

The white rose rested in her lap.

She should stand.

She should leave.

She should reclaim the sensible parts of herself before they vanished completely.

David crossed the room slowly.

Each step measured.

Controlled.

He stopped before her.

"Stay," he said.

Not casual.

Not command exactly.

Worse.

A request sharpened by need.

Ember's fingers closed around the rose.

Her pulse moved violently beneath her throat.

David heard it.

His eyes darkened.

For one breath, the apartment held its silence.

Then Ember looked up at him and said,

"Yes."

YOU WEAR THE DRESS for me.

You will pretend otherwise, but we are far beyond the mercy of pretending.

Black satin against your skin. Bare shoulders. Mouth dark enough to make every man in the room briefly stupid.

Including me.

Especially me.

When I open the door and see you holding the rose, I forget the first line I planned to say.

Do you understand how unforgivable that is?

No.

Not yet.

You enter my apartment, and the room sees immediately what I have tried, poorly, to contain.

That you know where to stand now.

That you no longer search for permission before touching the records or crossing toward the window.

That my attention finds you first, and yours rises to meet it.

Attachment has a scent.

The others notice.

Adrien notices because he was born to ruin restraint for sport.

Lucien notices because wisdom has made him inconvenient.

Thessa notices because she understands what it means to stand beside a beautiful monster and decide the danger is worth the warmth.

And Mateo notices because you are impossible not to notice.

He touches your hand.

Only that.

A polite greeting. Warm fingers. A compliment offered too smoothly by half.

Nothing unforgivable.

Except that your pulse changes.
Not for him.
Because of him.
Because I am there to hear it.
The glass cracks before I decide to crack it.
That is unfortunate.
Also, honest.
For one moment, the room sees me without the polish.
Good.
Let them remember.
Let him remember.
Let you remember.
Then you say my name.
David.
Softly.
Not afraid enough to leave.
Not foolish enough to miss what I am.
And I come back to myself because you asked me to.
Do you understand what power that is?
No.
Not yet.
But Adrien does.
Lucien certainly does.
Thessa begins to suspect.

And I, who have survived centuries without yielding control to anyone living or dead, stand in my own apartment with wine on my hand and obey the smallest correction in your voice.

You are making a mess.
Yes.
I am.
I have been making one since the night you arrived.
When I read the poem, I stop hiding the shape of my hunger.
Not the blood.
That truth waits with sharper teeth.
But the wanting.
The watching.
The restraint I have built around you like a cathedral contains hellfire.

You sit beneath my window with the rose in your lap, and I tell you in front of every witness who understands the language:

I will keep my hands open.

Until you step into them.

And when the room empties, I ask you to stay.

Not because I lack the power to keep you.

Because I want the answer from your own mouth.

You look up at me.

Your pulse is chaos.

Your eyes are not.

“Yes,” you say.

And the hunger in me lifts its head.

Chapter 9
After Midnight

The apartment changed after midnight.

Not visibly.

Nothing dramatic happened. The candles did not gutter out. The cemetery did not wake beneath the rain. No hidden doors opened beneath Marceaux House.

And yet, the moment the last guest disappeared down the stairwell, something in the rooms exhaled.

The performance ended.

What remained felt quieter.

Closer.

Dangerously real.

Rain slid steadily down the bay windows overlooking the cemetery, blurring marble angels into pale smears of silver and shadow. Vinyl spun low near the fireplace, the song reduced to soft piano and static crackle beneath the weather.

Ember still sat near the window with the white rose resting across her lap.

David stood several feet away, just inside the kitchen.

Too far.

Not far enough.

Neither of them spoke immediately.

The silence between them had evolved over the past week. It no longer felt uncertain. It felt inhabited. Like something living had settled inside it and made a home.

David removed the damaged wineglass from the kitchen sink and studied the fracture running through the crystal.

"You should throw that away," Ember said softly.

"I know."

He did not move to do it.

His fingers traced the crack once.

Then he set the glass down again with infuriating care.

Ember watched him in the candlelight.

Black shirt open slightly at the throat.

Silver rings.

Dark hair fallen loose now from whatever control he had imposed on it earlier.

Pale fingers still stained faintly red from spilled wine.

Something about him tonight looked thinner beneath the skin.

Less composed.

The realization sent a dangerous pulse of warmth through her stomach.

David glanced toward her immediately.

Her body had become readable to him.

God.

"You're staring again," he murmured.

Ember leaned one shoulder against the back of the velvet chair.

"You gave an entire room a poem about wanting me."

"One room."

"That feels like a technicality."

"It is."

The corner of her mouth lifted despite herself.

David watched that happen, too.

Always.

His gaze lingered on her mouth long enough that her pulse shifted again.

His eyes darkened instantly.

The room tightened.

"You hear everything, don't you?" she asked quietly.

"Not everything."

"That sounded suspiciously evasive."

"It was meant to."

Rain tapped softly against the windows.

David crossed toward the bay window slowly, stopping near enough that she could feel the subtle cold radiating from him again.

Not dead cold.

Winter-night cold.

Elegant cold.

The kind that invited touching purely to understand it.

Ember hated how often she thought about touching him now.

"I embarrassed Mateo," she said after a moment.

"You protected him."

The answer came too quickly.

Ember turned toward him.

David stood with one hand resting lightly against the chair beside her. His gaze remained on the cemetery below.

"You would have hurt him."

"Yes."

No hesitation.

No shame.

The honesty moved through her with the same dark heat his poetry did.

"You say terrifying things very calmly."

"I find panic theatrical."

"And threatening people isn't?"

A faint shadow of amusement crossed his mouth.

"He was not threatened."

Ember blinked slowly. "David."

This time he looked at her fully.

"He was warned."

The candlelight caught strangely in his eyes.

Not red.

Not unnatural.

Just darker than eyes should become from shadow alone.

Ember's throat tightened.

David noticed immediately.

Of course he did.

"You liked it," he said softly.

Her breath caught.

"What?"

"The attention."

Dangerous question.

More dangerous because it was true.

Not Mateo's attention.

His.

The possessiveness.

The quiet violence beneath his control.

The terrifying certainty of his focus.

Ember looked toward the rain-silvered windows instead of answering.

David stepped closer.

Only half a step.

Enough.

"You did," he murmured.

Not accusation.

Certainty.

The air between them thickened.

"You make it difficult to think clearly," Ember admitted quietly.

Something in David's expression shifted at that.

Not triumph.

Worse.

Hunger restrained too tightly.

"You think I remain clear-minded around you?"

The question entered her body like dark liquor.

"No," she whispered.

David's gaze lowered briefly.

To her mouth.

Her throat.

The line of bare skin above the neckline of her dress.

Then back to her eyes with visible effort.

There.

That was new.

Effort.

Ember felt it sharply now, the strain beneath his composure. Like something powerful pulling against chains hidden beneath silk and bone.

And suddenly she understood.

His restraint was not effortless elegance.

It was work.

Constant work.

The realization made her pulse stumble harder.

David closed his eyes briefly.

One breath.

Controlled.

Then another.

When he looked at her again, his voice had lowered further.

"You should not look at me that way tonight."

"Which way?"

"As though you're curious what happens when I stop behaving."

The words settled heavily between them.

Rain whispered harder against the glass.

Ember's heartbeat moved visibly now beneath her throat.

David stared at it.

Not subtly.

Not politely.

Stared.

The intensity of it turned her skin hot.

"David."

Her voice came softer than intended.

His jaw tightened immediately.

"Yes."

"You're doing it again."

"I know."

But he did not stop.

His gaze remained fixed on the pulse beneath her skin with unbearable concentration.

Ember swallowed once.

His eyes followed the movement.

The room seemed suddenly too warm despite the cold radiating from him.

Or perhaps she was simply overheating from the way he looked at her.

"Come here," he said quietly.

Not command.

Not request.

Need sharpened into sound.

Ember stood before she fully realized she intended to.

David watched her cross the small distance between them with frightening stillness.

The vinyl shifted into another song behind them.

Slower now.

Strings and low piano threading through candlelight.

Ember stopped directly before him.

Close enough to smell rain still lingering in his hair.

Close enough that her body recognized the cold surrounding his.

Neither touched.

Not yet.

David lifted one hand slowly.

Giving her time.

Always giving her time.

His fingers slid beneath her chin with exquisite care.

Cold skin against warm skin.

Ember inhaled sharply.

His thumb rested lightly near the corner of her jaw while his gaze searched her face with terrifying intensity.

Not lust alone.

Study.

Need.

Restraint fraying molecule by molecule.

"You make restraint feel unnatural," he said softly.

The confession nearly undid her.

Because it sounded involuntary.

Like truth dragged from him against his better judgment.

Ember's hands tightened against the fabric of her dress.

David noticed.

Of course.

He noticed everything.

"You rearrange my thoughts," he continued quietly. "My evenings. My instincts."

Her pulse fluttered violently beneath his hand.

His eyes darkened further.

"I hear your footsteps before you reach the hall."

The words wrapped around her slowly.

"I know when you've slept badly because your heartbeat changes the following night."

A faint shiver moved through her.

David's thumb shifted slightly against her jaw.

Careful.

Measured.

As though touch itself endangered him now.

"I begin records because I think you might come across the hall."

Ember's breathing had gone shallow.

The apartment blurred slightly at the edges.

Candles.

Rain.

Vinyl.

The cemetery glowing pale behind him.

David lowered his head incrementally closer.

Not enough.

Enough.

"And when you don't," he murmured, "the rooms feel wrong afterward."

The confession struck somewhere deep and ruinous inside her.

Because she understood exactly what he meant.

Her fingers lifted before she could stop herself.

David went perfectly still as her hand touched the center of his chest.

The fabric beneath her palm felt cool.

Not cold enough to repel.

Cold enough to fascinate.

She felt him inhale.

Sharp.

Controlled badly.

His eyes closed for one dangerous second.

That reaction alone nearly destroyed her composure.

"David," she whispered.

His hand moved suddenly.

Not rough.

Fast.

One arm sliding around her waist, pulling her closer with enough force to steal her breath.

Heat collided with cold.

Ember gasped softly as her body pressed against his.

David's restraint visibly fractured.

There was no other word for it.

His head lowered immediately toward her throat.

Not kissing.

Hovering.

Breathing her in with terrifying concentration.

Ember's entire body tightened.

His mouth stopped barely above her pulse.

One inch.

Less.

She could feel the shape of his breath against her skin now.

Cooler than human breath should be.

David's fingers flexed hard against her waist.

The pressure almost hurt.

Not quite.

The vinyl crackled softly behind them.

Rain hammered harder against the windows.

And Ember realized with growing, devastating clarity: he was trying not to bite her.

Not metaphorically.

Literally.

The knowledge should have frightened her.

Instead, heat spiraled violently through her stomach.

David made a low sound against her throat.

Not a growl.

Worse.

Need.

Raw and restrained and ancient enough to feel dangerous beneath her skin.

Ember tilted her head before she could think better of it.

Invitation.

The instant she did, David froze.

Every muscle in his body locked.

Silence exploded between them.

His mouth hovered against the line of her throat.

Then, slowly, agonizingly slowly, he lifted his head.

His eyes had changed.

Not dramatically.

But enough.

Darkness flooded them, nearly black now, pupils blown wide with hunger and something frighteningly close to panic.

Ember's breath caught.

David stared at her as if seeing the exact moment disaster became inevitable.

Then his gaze dropped to her mouth.

And for one terrible second, Ember knew he was going to kiss her.

She wanted him to.

God help her, she wanted him to.

His hand tightened around her waist.

His head lowered—

Then he vanished backward.

Not literally.

But fast enough to feel unnatural.

One moment his body surrounded hers.

The next he stood across the room beside the fireplace, breathing hard enough to expose the sharp rise and fall of his chest.

Distance crashed coldly between them.

Ember stared at him.

Rain roared outside now.

David braced one hand against the mantel with visible force.

The muscles in his jaw flexed sharply.

He would not look at her.

"David."

Her voice sounded wrecked.

He closed his eyes briefly.

"Do not," he said quietly.

The words carried a strain she had never heard from him before.

Ember's pulse still thundered beneath her skin where his mouth had almost touched her.

"You pulled away."

"Yes."

"Why?"

A harsh laugh escaped him.

Not amused.

Almost angry.

"Ember."

He finally looked at her again.

The hunger in his face stole what remained of her breath.

"Because another second," he said softly, "and I would not have."

Silence swallowed the apartment whole.

The vinyl continued spinning.

Candles trembled low against the storm.

And across the room, David Caesarius looked at her not like a man struggling with desire.

Like a predator starving beside an open throat.

YOU TILT YOUR HEAD for me.

Beautiful girl.

Do you understand what that gesture means to something like me?

No.

You only know that you wanted my mouth closer.

Wanted the danger acknowledged instead of hidden beneath manners and poetry and restraint polished smooth over centuries.

But I know.

I know exactly what it means when warm skin opens willingly beneath my gaze.

You touch my chest, and my entire body answers before thought can intervene.

The room disappears instantly.

No vinyl.

No candles.

No rain.

Only your pulse.

Only your throat beneath my mouth.

Only the impossible sweetness of you standing willingly inside my reach.

You ask if I think about you constantly.

Ember.

I have begun measuring nights by your footsteps in the hallway.

I know the difference between your exhausted breathing and your lonely breathing.

I know when you sketch because charcoal dust settles into the lines of your fingers.

I know when you stand at the cemetery window because your silhouette changes the light beneath your curtains.

You have entered my instincts.

That is the disaster.

Not desire.

Desire is simple.

This is infestation.

You make restraint feel unnatural because every civilized instinct in me has begun losing ground to older hungers.

When I pull you against me, your body fits with devastating ease.

Warmth.

Breath.

Heartbeat.

Living girl.

Mine.

The thought arrives viciously.

Uninvited.

Unforgivable.

And then you tilt your throat toward my mouth.

Invitation.

Trust.

Or ruinous curiosity.

Perhaps all three.

I lower my head because instinct finally outruns discipline.

One inch closer and I would have tasted you.

Not kissed.

Fed.

The truth of that nearly tears the remaining control from my hands.

So, I leave you.

Abruptly.

Violently.

Before hunger becomes action.

You look wounded when I step away.

God help me.

That almost sends me back to you.

You ask why I pulled away.

Because another second and I would not have.

Another second and your pulse would have opened beneath my mouth like a prayer answered at last.

And the worst part?

Some ancient, monstrous thing inside me believes you would have let it happen.

Chapter 10

Teeth Beneath Silk

Ember did not sleep.

That became obvious around four in the morning when she found suddenly herself standing barefoot at the cemetery window, still wearing the black satin dress from the salon.

Rain silvered the glass.

The Grant crypt gleamed pale beneath the magnolia tree, ghost-soft in the storm light. Somewhere below, water moved through iron drains with the sound of whispered voices.

Across the hall, silence.

No vinyl.

No footsteps.

No David.

Which should have relieved her.

Instead, the absence scraped against her nerves until she finally abandoned the window and crossed toward the kitchen.

The apartment felt too warm after being near him.

Or perhaps she had not recovered from the moment his mouth hovered against her throat while restraint visibly tore itself apart behind his eyes.

God.

Ember poured cold water into a glass and sipped.

Her pulse had finally steadied sometime around two.

Mostly.

Now and then her body remembered the pressure of David's hand at her waist and ruined the progress entirely.

She should leave Marceaux House.

A sane woman would already be packing.

Instead, Ember stood in her kitchen at four in the morning, replaying the exact sound David made against her throat before he stopped himself from biting her.

Not kissing.

Biting.

The distinction mattered now.

Too much.

A soft sound moved through the hallway outside.

Ember froze.

Not footsteps.

Too fast.

Like fabric whispering sharply across wood.

Then silence again.

Her stomach tightened.

The old building creaked softly around her. Rain tapped the windows. Somewhere downstairs a pipe groaned through the walls.

Nothing else.

Ember exhaled slowly.

"You're becoming paranoid," she muttered.

But even as she said it, she crossed toward the apartment door.

Carefully.

Quietly.

She looked through the peephole.

The hallway stood empty beneath amber sconces.

No movement.

No sound.

Still—

Something felt wrong.

Or watched.

Ember frowned and opened the door.

Cold air greeted her immediately.

The corridor stretched silent and narrow before her, rain-shadowed light spilling faintly through the cemetery window at the far end.

David's door remained closed.

No sound from within.

And yet—

Her eyes lifted slowly toward the ceiling.

The chandelier above the stairwell flickered slightly.

As though someone had disturbed it moments earlier.

Too quickly to hear.

A chill moved beneath her skin.

Impossible movement.

Ember stared toward David's apartment.

Then, slowly:

"David?"

No answer.

Of course not.

She almost closed the door again.

Then his voice drifted softly from behind her.

"You should not open doors at night without knowing who waits outside them."

Ember gasped hard enough to slam backward into the wall.

David stood inside her apartment.

Near the cemetery windows.

Black coat gone.

Black shirt open at the throat.

Rain still silvering faintly through the dark strands of his hair.

He had not been there seconds ago.

Her heartbeat exploded.

David's eyes closed briefly.

The reaction moved through him visibly.

Not pleasure.

Strain.

"You need to stop doing that," Ember breathed.

"You opened the door."

"That does not explain how you got behind me."

A pause.

David's gaze shifted toward the hallway beyond her shoulder.

Then back to her.

"It's late."

"That is not an answer."

"No."

He looked exhausted.

Not physically exhausted.

Controlled exhaustion.

Like restraint itself had become labor.

Ember closed the apartment door carefully.

Locked it.

Then turned toward him again.

"You disappeared. You just left me alone in your apartment."

His eyes darkened faintly at the words.

"I thought distance might improve the situation."

"And? Did it?"

"No."

The honesty hit her like heat.

David stood near the bay windows, watching her with unbearable focus.

Ember became abruptly aware that she still wore the black satin dress.

Still wore the earrings.

Still carried him all over her skin.

Dangerous realization.

"You moved too fast in the hallway," she said quietly.

His expression shifted almost imperceptibly.

Interesting.

So, she had not imagined it.

"You heard that?"

"I heard something."

David looked towards the rain outside.

"Old buildings distort sound."

"That was definitely not an answer."

A faint shadow touched his mouth.

"No."

The room quieted.

Rain moved against the glass in silver trails.

David's gaze drifted slowly over her face.

Then lower.

To the neckline of her dress.

To her throat.

Ember felt the attention physically now.

Like invisible fingertips.

"You should sleep," he said softly.

"You said that last time."

"And you ignored me last time as well."

"I'm beginning to think you enjoy giving impossible instructions."

His eyes returned to hers.

"I enjoy very little lately."

The words settled strangely between them.

Too honest.

Too tired.

Ember studied him carefully.

"There's something wrong with you tonight."

A silence entered him.

Not defensive.

Measured.

Dangerous.

"Yes."

No elaboration.

Of course.

Ember crossed slowly toward the kitchen counter, more to break the intensity than from actual thirst.

David tracked the movement immediately.

Always.

She reached automatically for the glass beside the sink.

"Ember."

The warning came instantly.

Too late.

Her fingers slipped against the crystal.

"Oh, damn it—"

The glass shattered against the counter.

Pain flashed sharp across her palm.

A bright line of blood welled instantly beneath her thumb.

Tiny injury.

Tiny.

The room changed anyway.

David appeared beside her so fast that the movement barely registered.

One second: distance.

The next: cold body against warmth.

His hand closed around her wrist with terrifying force.

Ember's breath caught.

David stared at the blood.

Not her hand.

The blood.

And everything inside him went still.

Not calm.

Predatory.

His pupils flooded dark instantly.

The apartment fell silent enough that Ember could hear rain striking the windows three rooms away.

David's grip tightened once.

Painfully.

Then loosened abruptly, as though he had remembered something important too late.

"David."

Her voice sounded thinner now.

His eyes lifted to hers.

Wrong.

Not red.

Not monstrous in some theatrical way.

Worse.

Hungry enough to erase the man almost completely.

Ember's pulse stumbled violently.

David heard it.

The reaction hit him visibly.

His jaw tightened hard enough to sharpen the bones beneath his skin.

"Go rinse it," he said quietly.

Not a suggestion.

A command dragged raw through restraint.

Ember did not move.

Fear should have arrived first.

Instead: heat.

Arousal.

Fascination.

Terror braided tightly together until she could no longer separate them.

David still loosely held her wrist.

His thumb rested directly beneath her pulse.

Cold.

Steady.

Dangerous.

"You're staring again," she whispered faintly.

His nostrils flared.

"You're bleeding."

The words sounded wrecked.

Like the scent itself was doing damage.

Ember's breathing shallowed.

"You're not human."

Silence.

"I mean, really ... not human."

Rain pattered against the windows.

"This is not make-believe."

Candles fluttered against an invisible wind.

"This is not a game."

Blood bright against pale skin.

David looked at her for one terrible, measured moment.

Then:

"No."

The truth entered the room softly.

No thunder.

No dramatic reveal.

Just honesty again.

Always honesty.

Ember should have pulled away.

Instead, she stepped closer.

David went perfectly still.

"Ember."

Warning.

Need.

Panic.

All at once.

"How old are you?" she asked quietly.

His gaze remained fixed on her bleeding hand.

"Older than your country."

A chill slid beautifully down her spine.

Impossible things.

Impossible speed.

Impossible stillness.

Impossible eyes.

And still she wanted him.

God help her.

David released her wrist abruptly and turned away.

Distance.

Sharp.

Immediate.

He braced both hands against the kitchen counter as if holding himself upright required concentration.

"You should be frightened now," he said quietly.

Ember stared at his back.

Broad shoulders.

Controlled breathing.

Violence buried beneath elegance.

"Are you going to hurt me?"

His laugh sounded terrible.

"No."

Too fast.

Too certain.

Ember's pulse jumped again.

David's head lowered.

One breath.

Another.

"I should leave this building," he said.

"You don't mean that."

"No."

The contradiction hung openly between them.

He should stay away from her.

He knew it.

And he wasn't leaving.

The realization moved through Ember with devastating heat.

David turned slowly toward her again.

His eyes remained dark.

Hungry.

Human enough to break her heart.

Monstrous enough to ruin it.

"I should stay away from you," he admitted softly.

"Then why don't you?"

Silence.

The rain intensified outside.

David looked at her like the answer offended him.

"Because I have wanted nothing this badly in a very long time."

The honesty nearly destroyed her.

Ember looked down at the blood still threading slowly across her palm.

David followed the movement instantly.

His entire body tightened.

There.

Again.

That visible strain.

As though instinct pulled against him hard enough to hurt.

Ember's voice lowered.

"What happens if I ask you not to stop?"

The words slipped out before caution could save her.

David froze completely.

The apartment stopped breathing.

Then slowly:

"Ember," his voice was an ache.

Her name sounded ruined in his mouth.

She stepped closer again.

One pace.

Enough.

David's control visibly fractured.

His eyes closed hard.

His throat moved once.

When he opened them again, hunger had flooded almost everything else away.

"Show me your hand."

The command came rough now.

Not elegant.

Ember lifted her palm slowly.

Blood glimmered dark against candlelight.

David stared at it with devastating concentration.

Then at her.

Asking silently.

Giving her one last chance to retreat.

Ember did not move.

David made a low sound deep in his chest.

Need.

Defeat.

Reverence.

Then he lifted her wrist carefully.

Cold fingers.

Warm skin.

His gaze never left hers as he lowered his mouth slowly toward the cut in her palm.

Ember's entire body tightened.

Not fear.

Anticipation.

David's lips brushed her skin first.

Soft.

Terribly soft.

Then his mouth closed over the wound.

The sensation shattered through her instantly.

Not pain.

Heat.

A sharp, intimate pull that traveled violently through her bloodstream and settled low in her stomach hard enough to steal breath from her lungs.

Ember gasped.

David's eyes closed.

A sound escaped him.

Not hunger now.

Relief.

Ancient and devastating.

His grip tightened around her wrist.

Not enough to hurt.

Enough to reveal how difficult gentleness had become.

Ember's knees nearly gave beneath her.

God.

David pulled away abruptly.

Too abruptly.

A single dark drop of her blood remained against his mouth.

The sight nearly ruined her.

He stared at her with naked horror.

And want.

Then at the blood on her palm.

Then back at her.

The apartment shook softly beneath distant thunder.

Neither moved.

Neither spoke.

And between them, the hunger finally had a shape.

You stand barefoot in your kitchen in the early hours of dawn, holding a bleeding hand as if it were a small, ordinary thing.

Beautiful girl.

You do not yet understand what blood does to a room like this.

To a creature like me.

The scent reaches me before the glass even hits the counter.

Sharp.

Warm.

Alive!

Everything inside me stops.

Not metaphorically.

Instinct strips civilization cleanly from my body in a single catastrophic second.

The rain disappears first.

Then the music.

Then thought itself.

Only you remain.

Your pulse.

Your skin.

The bright line of red welling slowly beneath your thumb.

God.

You look up when I reach you, startled by the speed of it, but not frightened enough. Never frightened enough around me.

That should comfort me.

Instead, it ruins me.

I take your wrist too hard.

Your heartbeat leaps violently beneath my hand.

Mine.

The thought arrives instantly.

Savage enough to blacken the edges of my vision.

I stare at the blood because if I look at your face right now, I may forget every civilized thing I have taught myself over centuries.

You say my name softly.

And I realize with horror that the sound of your voice makes the hunger worse.

Am I human?

No.

The truth slips loose too easily around you now.

No performance.

No careful lies.

Just hunger standing in your kitchen, breathing your blood into its lungs like a prayer pulls the power of God into one's soul.

You should run.

You should tear your wrist from my hand and flee this apartment and never return to the hallway that separates us.

Instead, you step closer.

Beautiful, ruinous girl.

Do you understand what courage smells like to a starving creature?

It smells warm.

Curious.

Devoted.

You ask how dangerous I am while your pulse stammers beneath my fingers like it already knows the answer.

More dangerous than you can imagine.

Less dangerous than I could become if you keep looking at me this way.

You stare at my mouth after I confess what I am.

Not revulsion.

Fascination.

God help me.

That is the moment I realize I am losing this war.

Because you are not recoiling from the monster.

You are watching him breathe.

And when you ask me what happens if you tell me not to stop...

Something ancient inside me nearly falls to its knees before you.

I lift your wrist carefully after that.

Trying to remember gentleness.

Trying to remember restraint.

Trying to remember that your body is breakable in ways mine no longer is.

You let me touch you.

That trust enters my bloodstream more violently than your blood ever could.

My mouth brushes your skin.

Your breath catches.

The sound tears through me.

Then I taste you.

Warm.

Living.

Catastrophically sweet.

Sweeter than anything I have tasted in my long existence.

Relief slams through my body hard enough to hurt.

Not appetite satisfied.

Need answered.

And suddenly I understand the genuine danger here has never been hunger.

It is this...

That somewhere between the rain and your ruined life and the white roses you carry in and out of the cemetery...

I have begun to belong to you too.

Chapter II
Hunger

The storm settled over New Orleans like a living thing.

By the next evening, rain drowned the streets in silver-black reflections and turned the cemetery beyond Marceaux House into a drowned kingdom of marble and iron. Thunder rolled low enough to vibrate through the building itself, while lightning flashed behind clouds thick as bruises.

Ember stood at her bay window with one sleeve pushed above her wrist.

The cut on her palm had already closed.

Not fully.

But faster than it should have.

She traced her fingertips slowly over the faint pink line beneath her thumb and tried not to think about David's mouth against her skin.

Failed immediately.

Heat moved through her body with humiliating ease now whenever she remembered him feeding from her hand.

Not feeding.

Tasting.

The distinction mattered.

Probably.

God.

Ember closed her eyes briefly.

The memory returned in brutal detail, anyway.

Cold fingers around her wrist.

His mouth soft against her palm.

The sound he made when her blood touched his tongue

Relief.

Not violence.

Solace.

That frightened her more than fangs would have.

A soft knock sounded at her door.

Not tentative.

Measured.

Her pulse reacted instantly.

Of course it did.

Ember crossed the apartment without bothering to ask who waited outside.

David stood in the hallway, wearing black from throat to wrist, rain still glimmering faintly along the shoulders of his coat.

His eyes dropped immediately to her uncovered hand.

Then lifted.

The room-temperature shift between them had become immediate now. Not metaphorical. Her body recognized him before thought caught up.

"You healed quickly," he said quietly.

No greeting.

No hello.

Only the wound.

Ember leaned one shoulder against the doorframe.

"You noticed."

"Yes."

"That doesn't surprise me anymore."

A shadow crossed his expression.

Not satisfaction.

Something closer to regret.

"May I come in?"

The formality of the question unsettled her.

Because she knew now.

He could probably enter without permission if he wished.

And yet he asked.

"Yes."

David crossed the threshold carefully.

Like the apartment itself had become dangerous territory.

Rain moved softly behind him in the hallway window before Ember closed the door again.

The silence that followed felt sharper than usual tonight.

Not comfortable.

Expectant.

David removed his coat slowly and draped it across the chair nearest the cemetery windows. Candlelight brushed the sharp lines of his face with gold and shadow.

He looked composed again.

Mostly.

But Ember had started recognizing the fractures now.

The slight tension in his jaw.

The too-careful stillness.

The way his breathing changed around her.

She noticed all of it.

Interesting.

Dangerous.

"You shouldn't have done that," he said quietly.

Ember turned toward him. "Done what?"

"Told me not to stop."

The words entered the room heavily.

No seduction layered over them tonight.

Only consequence.

Ember crossed slowly toward the kitchen counter.

"You seemed eager to obey me."

David's eyes darkened instantly.

"That is precisely the problem."

The storm cracked loudly outside.

Lightning flashed silver across the cemetery windows.

Ember folded her arms loosely.

"You could have hurt me."

"Yes."

The answer came too quickly.

Always honesty.

Her pulse jumped hard enough that David's gaze flicked toward her throat automatically.

There.

Again.

That impossible focus.

Ember watched him notice himself doing it.

Watched the restraint settle forcibly back into place.

"How dangerous are you?" she asked quietly.

David looked toward the rain-dark windows instead of answering immediately.

"More than you understand."

"And less than you fear?"

A faint shadow touched his mouth.

"Perhaps."

Ember moved closer before caution could intervene.

David stilled instantly.

The distance between them narrowed to breathing space.

"You said you're older than my country."

"Yes."

"How much older?"

"Enough that history begins repeating itself."

"That is infuriatingly vague."

"It is safer."

"For whom?"

His gaze lifted to hers slowly.

"You."

The answer should have frightened her.

Instead, warmth spiraled lower through her stomach.

There was something deeply wrong with her.

Or perhaps David Caesarius simply revealed the wrongness beautifully.

"You keep telling me to stay away from you," Ember said softly. "But you're the one standing in my apartment during a thunderstorm."

His eyes lowered briefly to her mouth.

"I am failing at distance."

The honesty of it wrecked something quiet inside her.

Ember reached for the edge of the counter behind her before her knees embarrassed her.

David noticed that too.

Of course.

"You're afraid," he murmured.

The words held fascination.

Not cruelty.

Ember swallowed once.

"Yes."

"And yet."

Not a question.

Certainty, once more.

Her pulse fluttered harder.

David's eyes darkened visibly.

"And yet," she admitted quietly.

The storm breathed against the windows.

Rain slid silver down the glass behind him while candlelight flickered low across the apartment.

Everything about the moment felt inevitable now.

Like the story had already chosen its direction long before either of them understood they were inside it.

"You should hate me for what I did last night," David said, his voice an ache of need.

Ember stared at him.

"You tasted my blood."

"Yes."

The word sounded rough.

Painful.

"And you looked horrified afterward."

A silence entered him.

Then.

"Because you liked it."

The truth landed brutally between them.

Ember's throat tightened.

David stepped closer immediately.

Instinct.

Predatory and helpless all at once.

"That," he said quietly, "is where this becomes dangerous."

Her breathing had gone shallow again.

David's gaze tracked it visibly.

"You wanted me to continue."

The accusation sounded almost anguished.

Ember looked away first, toward the rain.

Not because he was wrong.

Because he wasn't.

The memory of his mouth against her skin still lived low in her body like a fever refusing to break.

"I am not sure exactly what I want. I just know I should be more disturbed than I am," she whispered.

"Yes."

"And you should leave."

"Yes."

Neither moved.

Lightning flashed sharply outside.

David's control looked thinner tonight than ever before.

Not absent.

Breaking.

His hands flexed once at his sides as though resisting the urge to reach for her, physically hurt him.

Ember noticed that too.

"You're struggling," she said quietly.

His laugh came low and rough.

"Violently."

The answer moved through her with devastating heat.

God.

What was wrong with her?

David looked at her as if he already knew the answer.

"You are beginning to understand what I am," he said softly.

"No. I know what you are." Ember whispered in return. "Vampire."

The word settled into the room quietly.

No dramatic music.

No thunderclap.

Just truth.

David's expression did not change.

"Yes."

Ember should have recoiled.

Instead, she studied him harder.

Beautiful face.

Impossible eyes.

Stillness too precise to belong to anything human.

And beneath it all ... hunger.

Not metaphorical anymore.

Real.

Ancient.

Watching her like starvation taught elegance.

“You should run now,” David said. "And I should leave, while I still can."

“You keep saying that.”

“I keep meaning it.”

“But you don’t leave.”

His jaw tightened.

“No.”

The contradiction between them had become almost unbearable now.

Ember stepped closer again.

David inhaled sharply.

“Ember.”

Warning.

Need.

Prayer.

All inside her name.

“You’re afraid of yourself around me,” she said softly.

“Yes.”

“Because you might hurt me?”

His eyes closed briefly.

“When restraint breaks,” he said quietly, “I do not know how much of me remains civilized.”

The confession stole the breath from her lungs.

Not because it frightened her.

Because part of her wanted to see it.

That realization should have horrified her completely.

Instead, heat unfurled violently through her bloodstream.

David opened his eyes again.

One look at her face and he knew.

Of course, he knew.

The hunger inside him sharpened instantly.

“Do not look at me that way.”

"Which way?"

"As though the monster captures your attention more than the man."

The words cut unexpectedly deep.

Ember stepped directly into his space before fear could regain control.

"You think they're separate?"

David froze.

For one suspended second, the storm outside seemed to vanish entirely.

Then his hand closed around her wrist.

Too fast.

Too hard.

Ember gasped softly.

David looked down instantly as though only then realizing the force of his grip.

His eyes changed.

Darkness flooding outward.

Pupils blown wide.

Something ancient moving visibly beneath restraint.

His breathing turned uneven.

Not human uneven.

Predatory.

The apartment tightened around them.

David released her abruptly.

Too late.

The shape of his fingers already burned against her skin.

"I need to leave," he said quietly.

The words sounded wrecked.

Ember's pulse hammered violently.

Not fear.

Anticipation.

David heard it.

The effect nearly shattered what remained of his control.

He stepped backward sharply toward the cemetery windows.

Distance again.

Necessary distance.

Lightning illuminated him in brutal silver.

Black clothes.

Pale throat.

Eyes still wrong with hunger.

Beautiful enough to ruin religions.

"You should not want this," he said. "You should not want me."

But Ember looked at him standing against the storm like some starving dark thing dragged half out of myth and realized the truth with devastating clarity.

She did want him.

God help her.

She desired him so much that it made her ache.

And judging by the expression on David's face as he fought himself beside the rain-blackened windows—

He knew it too.

YOU SAY VAMPIRE ALOUD without trembling.

That should disturb me more than it does.

Instead, I feel relief.

Not because the truth is safe.

Because hiding it from you has become exhausting.

You stand in your apartment with storm light behind you and my bloodless hunger all over your skin, and you still step closer.

Beautiful girl.

Do you understand what courage looks like to something ancient?

It does not look like weapons.

Or prayers.

Or men with sharpened stakes, pretending bravery and fear, are different animals.

It looks like this.

A woman standing before a monster she should flee, asking for answers instead of mercy.

You ask how dangerous I am.

Ember.

Last night I tasted your blood and nearly lost the last civilized parts of myself around the sweetness of your pulse.

And tonight you move closer, anyway.

You should not.

God.

You should not.

But when you say vampire, there is a fascination in your voice beneath the fear.

Worse.

Desire.

That is the catastrophe.

Not that I hunger for you.

That was inevitable from the first night.

The catastrophe is that part of you hungers back.

Deeply.

You ask why I do not leave.

Because I am weak where you are concerned.

Because I have spent centuries mastering appetite only to discover you unravel discipline like silk sliding from skin.

Because I know exactly what will happen if restraint breaks completely.

And some monstrous part of me has begun wondering whether you would forgive it afterward.

When you step fully into my space, instinct overtakes thought.

My hand closes around your wrist too hard.

Your pulse jumps violently beneath my grip.

Mine.

The thought strikes instantly.

Savage.

Possessive enough to make my vision darken at the edges.

You gasp softly.

Not frightened enough.

That is the worst thing you could do to me.

I release you before hunger becomes action again.

Barely.

The room reeks now of rain, candle wax, storm electricity, and your blood beneath healing skin. Every sound inside your body reaches me too clearly.

Your heartbeat.

Your breathing.

The tiny shift in pulse when I tell you I must leave.

And then I hear it.

Not fear.

Desire.

You want the restraint to break.

Beautiful, ruinous girl.

You look at the monster and wonder what his mouth would feel like without mercy left in it.

And God help me.

Part of me wants to show you.

Chapter 12

The Invitation to Stay

David avoided her for two days.

Not completely.

That would have required absence.

And David Caesarius had become impossible for absence.

No vinyl drifted beneath her floorboards after midnight. No quiet knocks arrived at her window. No shadows crossed the cemetery balcony in the rain. He did not appear in the hallway when she left for coffee, nor on the stairwell when she returned carrying sketchbooks and groceries she barely remembered purchasing.

But Ember still felt him everywhere.

In the building.

In the silence.

Inside herself.

Marceaux House had learned his shape too well.

By Monday evening, the absence had become unbearable.

That realization should have frightened her more than it did.

Instead, it followed her through the apartment like a pulse.

She missed him.

Not despite the truth.

Because of it.

The knowledge of what he was had not broken the attraction. It had sharpened it into something feverish and magnetic and ruinously deliberate.

Vampire.

The word no longer sounded fictional in her mind.

It sounded like: cold fingertips, storm light, mouth against skin, eyes darkening with hunger, a beautiful man fighting himself beside cemetery windows

Ember stood at her bay window while rain softened the city beyond the crypts.

The storm had passed two nights earlier, but its remnants still haunted New Orleans in drifting mist and bruised clouds. Water gleamed silver along cemetery paths below, while magnolia branches swayed in the damp wind.

Across the hall: silence.

No music.

God.

Her body reacted to the absence now the way it once reacted to loneliness.

That thought landed hard enough to still her breathing.

"You're in trouble," she whispered to her reflection in the glass.

The cemetery offered no argument.

At ten forty-three, vinyl finally began.

Softly.

Almost cautiously.

A low cello first.

Then piano beneath it.

Ember closed her eyes.

Relief moved through her body with humiliating force.

She should ignore it.

Should let him keep his distance.

Should reclaim some remaining piece of sanity before David Caesarius consumed every quiet part of her life.

Instead, she crossed the apartment.

Barefoot.

Black sweater slipping loose from one shoulder.

Thin sleep shorts beneath it.

No makeup.

No armor.

The hallway glowed dimly beneath amber sconces as she stepped outside.

David's music moved beneath his door like memory returning to a room.

Ember stopped before it.

No invitation waited this time.

No rose.

No note.

Only silence and music and the shape of her own wanting.

Then she lifted her hand and opened the door herself.

The apartment beyond glowed low with candles.

David stood near the cemetery windows, holding a glass of red wine.

He turned instantly.

The moment he saw her, stillness entered him so completely it looked painful.

Neither spoke.

Rain whispered softly beyond the glass.

Vinyl crackled low beneath the cello.

Candles burned gold against black walls and old books.

David's gaze crawled over her.

Bare legs.

Oversized sweater.

Loose hair.

Bare mouth.

No performance tonight.

No black satin dress.

No poetry salon elegance.

Something in his expression changed.

Not hunger first.

Something more dangerous.

Tenderness.

"You came across the hall," he said quietly.

The words sounded almost disbelieving.

Ember closed the door behind herself.

"Yes."

David watched her carefully.

Not moving.

Not approaching.

As though any sudden motion might fracture the fragile, impossible thing happening between them.

"You should not be here," he murmured.

"You keep saying that."

"And you keep ignoring me."

Ember crossed slowly toward the center of the room.
The apartment felt different tonight.
Less theatrical.
More intimate.
No audience.
No velvet performance of civility.
Only rain and records and the impossible gravity between them.
"You disappeared," she said softly.
David's jaw tightened.
"I tried."
"Why?"
His eyes lowered briefly.
"To give you distance from this."
"This," Ember repeated quietly.
His gaze lifted to hers again.
"Me."
The honesty still ruined her.
Even now.
Especially now.
Ember stopped a few feet away from him.
Close enough to feel the cold surrounding his body.
Close enough to smell wine and rain, and David himself.
"You think knowing what you are would send me running."
"Yes."
"But it didn't."
"No."
A strange silence settled between them.
David looked exhausted again.
Not physically.
Hungry exhaustion.
Like resisting himself had become a war fought minute by minute.
"You missed me."
The words slipped out before Ember could stop them.
David closed his eyes briefly.
One measured breath.
Then another.
"Yes."

The answer entered her bloodstream like heat.

No games.

No evasion.

Always truth.

Ember's pulse fluttered hard enough that his gaze dropped instantly toward her throat.

There it was again.

That unbearable focus.

Only now she understood exactly what lived inside it.

And instead of recoiling—

God help her.

She stepped closer.

David went completely still.

"Ember."

Warning again.

But weaker now.

She could hear it.

"You keep walking toward the thing that could ruin you," he said softly.

The line should have sounded frightening.

Instead, it sounded wrecked.

Ember lifted her eyes to his.

"You keep asking me not to."

Something inside him visibly gave way.

Not entirely.

Enough.

David crossed the remaining distance in one smooth movement.

His hand closed carefully around her waist.

Cold palm against warm skin beneath the sweater.

Ember inhaled sharply.

The reaction moved through him instantly.

His eyes darkened.

Not monstrous yet.

Hungry.

Need sharpened into restraint.

"You should be afraid of me tonight," he murmured.

"Are you afraid of yourself tonight?"

"Yes."

The answer came rough.

Immediate.

Ember's heart stumbled hard enough that his fingers tightened reflexively at her waist.

David lowered his head slowly.

Giving her time.

Giving her space.

Giving her one last chance to retreat.

She didn't.

His mouth touched her throat softly.

The sensation shattered through her.

Not a kiss at first.

A lingering brush of cold lips against a warm pulse.

Reverent.

Devastating.

Ember's fingers closed suddenly in the front of his black shirt.

David made a low sound against her skin.

Need.

Relief.

Hunger.

All braided together.

His mouth moved higher slowly beneath her jaw.

Kissing now.

Openly.

Each touch careful enough to feel dangerous.

Ember tilted her head instinctively.

Invitation.

David's control faltered visibly.

His hand flexed hard at her lower back, pulling her closer until warmth and cold collided fully between them.

The contrast wrecked her.

God.

The room smelled like...

Rain.

Wine.

Wax.

His skin.

Her pulse.

David's breathing had gone uneven again.

Predatory.

He pressed his forehead briefly against hers as though trying to steady himself through contact.

The gesture felt almost unbearably intimate.

"You are making this impossible," he whispered.

Ember's hands slid upward into his hair before caution could stop her.

Soft dark strands tangled instantly between her fingers.

David froze.

Then shuddered.

Actually shuddered.

The reaction alone nearly destroyed her composure.

"You like that," she breathed softly.

His eyes lifted slowly to hers.

"Ember."

No denial.

Only warning.

Her pulse hammered harder.

David heard it.

The hunger sharpened immediately behind his eyes.

His mouth lowered toward her throat again.

Slower this time.

Intentional.

Not losing control.

Choosing.

Ember's entire body tightened in anticipation.

His lips brushed the pulse beneath her jaw once.

Twice.

Then stopped.

Hovering.

Breathing her in.

"Tell me to stop," he said quietly.

The words sounded pained.

Like he needed the refusal because he could no longer trust himself to create one.

Ember's fingers tightened slightly in his hair.

"No."
The answer broke something.
David's eyes closed hard.
Then his mouth moved toward her wrist instead.
Safer.
Barely.
He lifted her hand carefully between both of his.
Cold fingers surrounding warmth.
The contrast felt addictive now.
He turned her wrist slowly beneath the candlelight.
The healed cut remained faintly visible beneath her thumb.
David stared at it with devastating concentration.
Then looked at her once more.
Asking.
Always asking, even now.
Ember nodded once.
That was all it took.
David lowered his mouth to her wrist.
The kiss came first.
Soft.
Lingering.
Almost worshipful.
Then his lips parted carefully against her pulse.
A sharp ache followed.
Not pain exactly.
Pressure.
Heat.
Intimacy so intense it nearly blurred her vision.
Ember gasped softly.
David's eyes closed instantly.
Relief moved visibly through him this time.
Not violent hunger.
Something deeper.
More dangerous.
Need answered.
His grip tightened around her hand while he fed slowly from her wrist.
The room dissolved around the edges.

Rain.

Candles.

Music.

Everything distant now compared to the feeling of his mouth against her skin and the terrifying tenderness inside the restraint he still fought to maintain.

Ember's knees weakened.

David pulled away immediately.

A dark drop of blood marked his mouth.

Beautiful.

The thought entered her before shame could stop it.

David looked at her with naked hunger, and something almost broken beneath it.

"You should not trust me this much," he whispered.

But Ember stepped closer again, anyway.

David's entire body reacted.

There.

That visible fracture in control again.

His hand slid against the back of her neck instinctively, fingers threading into her hair as though resisting the urge to pull her fully against him required effort.

"You keep asking me to leave," she murmured softly.

"Yes."

"But you don't want me to."

The truth moved visibly across his face.

Slowly.

Terribly.

"No."

Rain moved silver down the cemetery windows behind him.

The vinyl shifted softly into another song.

David stared at her like he no longer remembered how distance worked.

Then quietly:

"Stay tonight."

The words entered the room like confessions.

Not casual.

Not temporary.

Loaded with everything he had failed to deny since the night she first crossed his threshold.

Ember felt her pulse flutter hard beneath her skin.

David heard that, too.

Of course he did.

And still, he waited.

Still gave her the choice.

Ember lifted one hand slowly to his face.

Cold skin beneath warm fingertips.

Beautiful monster.

Mine, some dangerous part of her thought suddenly.

The realization stole the breath from her lungs.

Then she whispered, "Yes."

YOU OPENED MY DOOR without an invitation.

Beautiful girl.

Do you understand what that means to something ancient?

Not politeness.

Not courage.

Choice.

You stand in my apartment dressed for sleep instead of seduction, and somehow the intimacy of that destroys me faster than black satin ever could.

Bare legs.

Loose sweater.

No armor.

You came to me as yourself tonight.

That is infinitely worse.

I attempted distance for forty-eight hours.

Forty-eight catastrophic hours without your footsteps in the hall, without your pulse beneath my windows, without the possibility of your voice crossing my rooms after midnight.

The apartment noticed your absence.

So did I.

When you step inside, I realize immediately.

You are no longer tolerating danger.

You are choosing it.

Me.

God.

You choose me.

You ask why I disappeared.

Because restraint was easier before you started walking willingly toward the monster.

Before you looked at hunger and answered it with curiosity instead of fear.

You stand close enough that your warmth reaches me in waves.

Your pulse is restless tonight.

Wanting.

Uncertain.

But not afraid enough.

Never afraid enough.

When I touch your waist, your body yields instantly.

Not submission.

Desirous certainty.

As though your skin already understands mine.

You tilt your throat toward my mouth again.

Do you know what trust smells like to a vampire?

It smells warm.

Sweet.

Ruinous.

I kiss your skin because it is safer than feeding.

Then you place your hands in my hair, and every remaining civilized thought inside me fractures at once.

You do not understand what that gesture does to me.

No one has touched me gently in a very long time.

Not gently.

Not without fear beneath it.

But your fingers move through my hair like affection instead of caution.

The hunger in me nearly becomes something else entirely.

Something softer.

More dangerous.

When I ask you to tell me to stop, I am giving both of us mercy.

You deny it immediately.

No.

Such a small word.

Such catastrophic permission.

So I take your wrist instead of your throat.

The safer hunger.

Though barely.

I feed carefully.

Slowly.

Trying to make devotion stronger than appetite.

Your blood reaches my mouth, and relief moves through me so violently I nearly pull you against me hard enough to bruise.

Need answered.

That is what you have become.

Not temptation.

Not fascination.

Necessary.

You should run the moment you realize that.

Instead, you step closer again.

And when I ask you to stay tonight, I hear the truth beneath my own voice clearly for the first time.

It is not lust speaking.

Not even hunger.

It is loneliness finally finding a shape it cannot bear to lose.

Chapter 13
Velvet Hunger

Ember woke tangled in black silk sheets to the sound of rain.

For one disoriented moment, she did not recognize the ceiling above her.

Dark wood beams.

Candlelight burned low somewhere beyond her vision.

Vinyl crackled softly through the apartment.

Then memory returned all at once.

David's mouth against her wrist.

Cold hands in her hair.

Stay tonight.

Heat moved instantly through her body.

God.

Ember pushed herself upright slowly.

The bed beneath her felt impossibly decadent; all dark linens and heavy velvet blankets carrying the faint scent of David himself.

Clove smoke.

Old paper.

Rain.

Something colder beneath it all.

The room remained dim except for scattered candles and silver-blue dawn filtering faintly through the cemetery windows.

She had fallen asleep in his bed.

Not beside him.

That realization arrived second.

Ember looked toward the empty space beside her.

Cold sheets.

Undisturbed.

A strange ache moved through her chest before she could stop it.

Then she heard the piano.

Soft.

Slow.

Down the hall.

Ember slipped from the bed barefoot, still wearing the oversized black sweater from the night before. The hem brushed high against her thighs as she crossed the room toward the doorway.

David's apartment looked different at dawn.

Less theatrical.

More haunted.

Candles guttered low beside overflowing bookshelves while rain painted silver trails down the massive cemetery windows. The city beyond them still slept beneath fog and storm light.

And there—

David sat at the small piano near the bay window.

Black shirt rolled up at the forearms.

Dark hair falling loose around his face.

Long, pale fingers moving slowly across ivory keys.

He looked ancient in moments like this.

Not old.

Ancient.

As if the music had survived inside him longer than entire civilizations.

Ember stopped in the doorway quietly.

David spoke without turning.

"I watched you sleep for almost eleven minutes before leaving the bedroom."

Her pulse jumped instantly.

"You counted?"

"Yes."

"That's concerning."

"I know."

A faint smile touched her mouth.

David finally looked over his shoulder.

The moment his gaze found her, the music faltered briefly beneath his hands.

Not enough for most people to notice.

Enough for her.

Interesting.

His eyes lingered on her bare legs beneath the sweater.

Then upward.

The hunger remained there.

Always there now.

But softer this morning.

No.

Not softer.

Fed.

The realization tightened low in her stomach.

Ember crossed toward him slowly.

"You play beautifully," she said quietly.

David's gaze lingered on her mouth one dangerous second before returning to the piano.

"I've had time to practice."

"That may be the most immortal thing you've said so far."

The corner of his mouth shifted faintly.

Ember stopped beside the piano bench.

Close enough that cold drifted gently from his skin again.

She had begun associating that coldness with comfort.

That realization should have terrified her.

Instead, her body relaxed instinctively near it.

David noticed.

Of course he did.

"You slept deeply," he murmured.

"I was tired."

"You were calmer afterward."

The words settled between them heavily.

Afterward.

After feeding.

Heat rose beneath Ember's skin.

David watched it happen.

"Does that disturb you?" he asked quietly.

Ember should say yes.

Instead...

"No."

His hands stilled completely against the piano keys.

Rain whispered harder against the windows.

"That at least should concern you," he said softly.

"It does."

"But not enough."

"No."

The honesty moved visibly through him.

Not triumph.

Relief.

Dangerous relief.

Ember leaned lightly against the piano.

"You're different today."

David looked at her carefully.

"How?"

"You're not pretending this is a secret to be hidden anymore."

Silence as he gazed at her gently.

Then he replied, "No."

The single word entered her bloodstream like wine.

Possessive warmth curled low through her body before she could stop it.

Mine.

The thought came suddenly again.

Not fully formed.

Not reasonable.

But there.

David's gaze sharpened immediately.

Her pulse betrayed her before her face could.

God.

"You should not think things that loudly around a vampire," he murmured.

Ember stared at him.

"You can't read minds."

"No."

"Then how—"

"You breathe differently when you want something."

Heat flooded her face.

David's eyes darkened instantly.

Interesting.

Dangerous.

He stood slowly from the piano bench.

Tall.

Elegant.

Predatory in ways that no longer hid fully beneath civility.

His hand settled on her lower back automatically when he stepped close.

Possession through instinct.

Ember noticed that now, too.

The guiding touch.

The territorial positioning.

The way he always moved her closer to him rather than away.

"My Ember."

The words slipped out quietly.

Not theatrical.

Not intentional.

Worse.

Natural.

The room went still around them.

David seemed to realize what he had said only after the silence arrived.

Ember's pulse jumped violently.

His eyes closed briefly.

"David."

His gaze lifted slowly to hers.

Something vulnerable moved beneath the hunger for one fleeting second.

Then disappeared again.

"You should tell me to stop saying things like that."

"But you don't want me to."

No answer.

Only that unbearable look again.

Want sharpened into restraint.

A knock sounded suddenly at the apartment door.

David went still instantly.

Not surprised.

Annoyed.

Interesting.

He looked toward the hallway with visible irritation before stepping away from her.

Losing his hand at her back felt immediate.

Wrong.

God.

Ember hated how quickly her body noticed the absence.

David crossed toward the door while she remained beside the piano, trying unsuccessfully to steady her pulse.

He opened the door.

Adrien Avenoire leaned casually against the frame, holding a clove cigarette between elegant fingers.

"Well," Adrien drawled immediately, eyes flicking toward Ember in David's apartment wearing only the oversized sweater. "This is becoming deliciously domestic."

David's expression flattened.

"What do you want?"

Adrien smiled slowly.

"Brunch invitations. Emotional devastation. Perhaps a front-row seat to your self-control collapsing in real time."

"You've had the last one for weeks."

"True." Adrien's gaze drifted toward Ember again. "Though I admit I underestimated her."

David shifted slightly.

Tiny movement.

Enough to partially block Adrien's view of her.

Possessive.

Openly now.

Adrien noticed instantly.

His smile widened.

"Oh," he murmured. "There it is."

"Adrien."

Warning.

Mild.

Dangerous.

The other vampire exhaled smoke lazily into the hallway.

"You know Lucien believes you're becoming irrational."

"I don't care."

That answer came too fast.

Adrien blinked once.

Then laughed softly.

"My God. You really are gone."

David's jaw tightened.

Ember crossed slowly toward them before the conversation sharpened further.

Adrien's eyes flicked immediately toward the faint mark near her wrist where feeding had bruised lightly beneath pale skin.

His smile vanished.

Not fully.

Enough.

"Well," he said softly. "That escalated."

David's hand closed instantly around Ember's waist, pulling her lightly against his side.

Not violent.

Claiming.

The gesture sent heat spiraling through her body with devastating speed.

Adrien noticed that too.

Interesting.

"You marked her already," Adrien murmured.

David's fingers flexed possessively once against Ember's hip.

"Yes."

The room-temperature shift happened instantly.

No pretending now.

No subtle implication.

Possession entered the room openly.

Adrien studied them both carefully.

Then his attention landed on Ember.

"You understand what this means?"

David answered before she could.

"She understands enough."

The possessive language struck low and hot inside her.

Mine.

My Ember.

She understands enough.

This should disturb her more.

Instead, her body softened instinctively into David's touch.

God.

Adrien saw that too.

The amusement faded slowly from his expression.

"Ah," he murmured quietly. "That's worse."

David's gaze sharpened instantly.

"Explain."

Adrien flicked ash into the hallway.

"She likes it."

Silence.

Devastating silence.

Because it was true.

David looked down at Ember slowly.

His hunger changed visibly.

Not sharper.

Deeper.

Something dark and reverent moving beneath it now.

Ember's pulse stumbled hard enough that his fingers tightened automatically against her waist.

Adrien looked suddenly less amused.

And slightly concerned.

"Well," he said lightly. "This feels catastrophic. I'm leaving before one of you makes it weirder."

"You arrived specifically to make it worse," Ember pointed out.

"Yes," Adrien agreed. "But now it's becoming emotionally sincere, and that's exhausting."

David shut the door in his face.

The apartment fell quiet again.

No rain.

No piano.

No vinyl.

Cold fingers still spread possessively against Ember's waist.

Neither moved immediately.

Then David took her hand and lowered his head slowly toward the feeding mark on her wrist.

His mouth brushed the bruise softly.

Ember inhaled sharply.

The reaction moved visibly through him.

"There," he murmured quietly against her skin. "That."

"What?"

His eyes lifted to hers.

"The way your pulse changes now."

Heat spiraled violently through her.

David's gaze darkened.

"You associate me with comfort already."

The words sounded almost horrified.

Not because he disliked it.

Because he liked it too much.

Ember swallowed once.

"You make it sound manipulative."

"It is."

Honesty again.

Always honesty.

"We both realize on some level, that you already know this ... And yet," he murmured softly, "you come."

His mouth lowered once more to the inside of her wrist.

Kissing now.

Slowly.

Lingering.

Ember's knees weakened instantly.

David felt it.

His arm tightened around her waist automatically, steadying her against him.

"You should not trust hunger this much," he whispered against her pulse.

But his voice lacked conviction now.

Because he trusted it too.

Ember's fingers curled slowly into the front of his shirt.

"It's stopped feeling like appetite."

David went still.

Then very carefully he replied, "Yes."

The word sounded dangerous.

"What does it feel like now?"

His eyes closed briefly.

When he answered, his voice had roughened into something almost painful.

"Necessary."

The word entered her body like heat beneath skin.

Necessary.

Not wanted.

Not desired.

Needed.

David looked at her as though the confession itself frightened him.

"You have become part of my instincts," he admitted quietly. "Part of my nights. My restraint. My thoughts." His thumb brushed slowly across her wrist. "Feeding from you no longer feels like hunger being satisfied."

Ember's breathing had gone shallow again.

David's eyes darkened immediately.

"It feels," he whispered, "like something in me settling when you're near."

God.

The room blurred softly around the edges.

Rain moved silver across cemetery glass while candles flickered low through the apartment.

And suddenly Ember understood.

This was no longer seduction.

It was an attachment becoming irreversible.

David lowered his mouth slowly toward her wrist again.

Not asking this time.

Not because consent vanished.

Because it already existed between them now, like breath.

His lips parted carefully against her pulse.

The ache bloomed deeper this time.

Longer.

Not painful.

Intimate enough to feel devastating.

Ember gasped softly and clutched harder at his shirt as warmth spiraled through her bloodstream in slow, violent waves.

David's eyes closed instantly.

Relief again.

Need answered.

His grip on her waist tightened possessively while he fed from her with unbearable restraint and terrifying tenderness.

And this time—

Ember realized she never wanted him to stop.

YOU SLEEP IN MY bed.

Beautiful girl.

Do you understand how dangerous tenderness becomes to something ancient?

Hunger is manageable.

Lust is manageable.

Violence is manageable.

Tenderness is catastrophe.

You wake slowly beneath the scent of rain and old records, and when you walk toward the piano half-dressed and barefoot, something in me reacts with immediate territorial instinct.

Mine.

The thought arrives effortlessly now.

That should alarm me more.

Instead, I wonder how quickly I can make the apartment feel like yours too.

You relax near my cold skin this morning.

Not despite it.

Because of it.

That realization nearly undoes me.

You have associated my hunger with safety.

Do you understand what that means?

No.

Not yet.

But your body does.

Your pulse steadies when I touch you now. Your breathing deepens after feeding. You lean unconsciously toward my voice when I move through the room.

You are bonding with the monster.

And God help me.

I am bonding back.

When Adrien arrives, he smells it instantly.

Blood.

Attachment.

Possession.

He looks at the mark on your wrist and realizes before speaking another word that I have already crossed lines I swore not to cross.

Then I touch your waist in front of him.

Not calculated.

Instinct.

Claim.

You soften into the touch immediately.

That reaction strikes every predatory instinct inside me with devastating force.

Because you like it.

You like being held this way.

Claimed this way.

Watched this way.

And suddenly I understand with terrifying clarity that if I asked you to stay forever tonight—

You might say yes.

The thought nearly starves me.

When I tell you feeding has become necessary, it is the closest thing to a confession I have spoken in centuries.

Necessary.

You have become part of my instincts now.

Part of the architecture of my restraint.

The records begin because of you.

The nights shape themselves around you.

My body recognizes your presence before thought catches up.

And when I feed from your wrist again, slower this time, I realize the final, terrible truth beneath all the hunger and obsession and need.

I no longer know where appetite ends and devotion begins.

CHAPTER 14

THE CATHEDRAL OF HUNGER

BY THURSDAY NIGHT, THE cemetery at night no longer frightened Ember.

That realization arrived quietly while she stood beneath rain-dark magnolia branches, watching candlelight flicker through the stained-glass windows of the small chapel next to the cemetery.

The fear had dissolved somewhere between David's mouth on her wrist and the way his hands settled instinctively against the small of her back whenever another vampire entered a room.

Now the cemetery felt almost sacred.

A threshold.

A place where the dead waited patiently beneath marble while the living wandered dangerously close to becoming eternal themselves.

Rain misted softly through the cemetery paths tonight, silvering the black lace of Ember's coat and dampening the ends of her dark auburn hair. Gas lamps glowed low along the pathways, throwing gold against crypt walls older than entire American cities.

David walked beside her in silence.

Black wool coat.

Dark gloves.

Elegant stillness.

And yet she had learned by now:

David was never truly still.

Not around her.

The hunger moved constantly beneath him.

Breathing.

Watching.

Restraining itself.

His hand rested low against her spine as they walked between the crypts.

Possessive now without apology.

Ember liked it far too much.

"You wanting to come with me to this cemetery feels strange," she murmured.

David glanced toward her.

"You live beside it."

"That sounds suspiciously evasive."

"It is."

A faint smile touched her mouth.

The cemetery stretched around them in pale stone and rain-shadowed angels while thunder rolled softly over New Orleans beyond the iron gates.

David guided her toward the Grant crypt slowly.

Not steering.

Claiming direction.

Ember noticed every small, instinctive thing now.

The hand on her back.

The way he always positioned himself between her and strangers.

The subtle lowering of his voice when he said her name.

Mine.

The thought moved through her again.

No longer shocking.

Dangerous how quickly it had begun feeling natural.

The Grant crypt rose before them in white marble-streaked silver beneath rainwater. Ivy crawled slowly along one side while weathered angels stood guard above the entrance.

David stopped there.

His gaze lifted toward the carved family name above the door.

"Your great-grandfather loved you very much."

The softness in his voice startled her.

"You didn't know him."

"No."

"But you say that as if you knew him."

David's eyes lowered slowly to hers.

"I knew men like him."

Silence settled between them.

Rain whispered softly over the stone.

Then David reached toward the crypt door.

Ember blinked. "You can get inside?"

A shadow crossed his mouth.

"Ember."

Right.

Vampire.

Ancient vampire.

Breaking into mausoleums probably ranked low on his moral crisis list.

The old iron lock gave easily beneath his hand.

The crypt opened with a low groan of ancient hinges.

Cool air drifted outward, smelling faintly of stone, candle wax, and rain-damp earth.

Ember stepped inside first, and dim light suddenly exploded from the interior as she felt a rush of power pass her.

The crypt glowed softly beneath dozens of old prayer candles, now burning low against the walls. Marble shelves lined both sides of the chamber, while stained glass overhead filtered storm light wine-red and gold across the floor.

The entire room felt suspended outside of time.

David entered behind her.

The heavy door closed softly.

The sound echoed.

Private.

Final.

Ember turned slowly beneath the colored light.

"This feels like a cathedral."

David watched her carefully.

"In some ways, it is."

The answer moved strangely through her.

Not metaphorical.

Honest.

The realization tightened something low in her chest.

David slowly removed his gloves.

Pale fingers.

Silver rings.

Predatory elegance sharpened by candlelight.

Then he crossed toward her.

Leisurely.

Inevitable.

His hand settled against the side of her throat, gently enough to feel reverent.

Ember's pulse jumped instantly beneath his palm.

David closed his eyes briefly.

The reaction moved visibly through him now, every time.

Need answered.

Need worsened.

Both simultaneously.

"You should not bring me somewhere this intimate," she whispered.

"You stopped being separate from intimate things a long time ago."

The words entered her body like heat.

David's thumb brushed slowly beneath her jaw.

"Do you know what happens," he said quietly, "when a vampire chooses someone permanently?"

The air inside the crypt changed.

Not colder.

Heavier.

Ember's breathing slowed.

"You mean turning someone?"

"No."

The answer came immediately.

More serious than that.

David studied her face for one long moment before continuing.

"There are vampires who feed casually. Carelessly. They survive on appetite alone." His gaze lowered briefly to her throat. "And there are others who bind themselves to one person until death becomes irrelevant."

A slow chill moved beautifully down Ember's spine.

"Bind," she repeated softly.

"Yes."

The word sounded ancient in his mouth.

"Like marriage?"

Something vulnerable crossed his face then.

Not weakness.

Worse.

Truth.

"More permanent."

Ember's pulse stumbled hard beneath his hand.

David heard it instantly.

Of course he did.

"You're serious."

"Yes."

Lightning flashed faintly through the stained-glass overhead.

Red and gold light spilled across David's face in fractured pieces while rain moved softly upon the crypt roof.

"And what happens?" Ember asked quietly.

His jaw tightened.

The immortal mask cracked there for one brief, dangerous moment.

Fear.

Not for himself.

For her.

"The vampire begins centering their existence around the chosen person." His voice lowered further. "Their instincts change. Hunger changes. Separation becomes..." He stopped briefly. "Unpleasant."

Ember almost laughed softly at the understatement.

David's eyes darkened.

"I am trying to speak carefully."

"Why?"

"Because I do not want you to hear obsession where I mean devotion."

God.

The honesty nearly ruined her.

David's hand slid slowly from her throat into her hair.

Cold fingers threading gently through dark auburn strands.

The intimacy of the gesture tightened her entire body.

"I have existed a very long time, Ember."

"I know."

"No," he said softly. "You know the number. You do not understand the weight."

The candlelight trembled around them.

David looked at her with terrifying openness now.

No polished restraint.

No elegant distance.

Only a man who had stopped hiding how deeply she reached inside him.

"I have fed from thousands of people."

The words struck harder than they should have.

Not jealousy.

Perspective.

Time.

Immortality measured in bodies and centuries.

David's gaze sharpened immediately at her reaction.

"But I have never wanted permanence with anyone before."

Silence flooded the crypt.

The confession landed between them like something sacred and ruinous all at once.

"Not once?" Ember whispered.

"No."

The answer sounded almost angry with its own honesty.

David stepped closer.

Their bodies nearly touched now.

Rain moved softly overhead while candles burned low around marble and stained glass.

"You are the only person who has ever made eternity feel frightening to me."

Ember's breath caught.

David lowered his forehead slowly against hers.

The contact shattered something quiet inside her chest.

Because he sounded terrified.

Not of hunger.

Not of losing control.

Of loving her enough to lose her.

"You're afraid I'll die," she whispered.

His entire body went still.

Then.

"Yes."

The word barely existed.

Ember's chest tightened painfully.

For the first time since meeting him, she understood the true scale of immortality.

Not endless life.

Endless grief.

David's hand trembled faintly in her hair.

Tiny movement.

Enough to devastate her.

Immortal creature.

Ancient predator.

Hands shaking because of her.

God.

Ember kissed him first.

Not careful anymore.

Not hesitant.

Her mouth found his with enough force to pull a low sound from deep in his chest instantly.

Need.

David's restraint shattered visibly.

His hands closed around her waist hard enough to steal breath as he pulled her fully against him.

Cold.

Heat.

Rain-damp wool.

Hungry mouths.

The kiss deepened immediately.

No polite restraint left now.

David kissed like starvation wrapped in worship.

Ember's fingers tangled fiercely into his hair while his mouth moved against hers with terrifying precision and growing desperation.

The crypt blurred around them.

Candles.

Rain.

Marble saints.

Everything dissolved beneath the feeling of David Caesarius finally kissing her without pretending he could survive distance anymore.

His body trembled against hers.

Actual trembling.

Ember felt it.

David seemed to realize she felt it too because a rough sound escaped him before his mouth left hers abruptly.

His head lowered instantly against her throat instead.

Breathing uneven now.

Predatory.

"David."

Her voice sounded wrecked.

His hands tightened hard around her waist.

Too hard.

The hunger surged visibly beneath his skin.

Ember felt it in the way he held her.

The way his breathing roughened.

The way his mouth hovered against her pulse like restraint had become physically painful.

Then his teeth grazed her throat.

Sharp.

Barely there.

Her entire body arched instantly against him.

God.

David made a ruined sound low in his chest.

The reaction nearly destroyed him.

"You should not react that way," he whispered against her skin.

But Ember realized the devastating truth now as clearly as the candlelight surrounding them.

She wanted the monster too.

Not despite the hunger.

Because of it.

Because the danger lived inside the devotion.

Because the possession sharpened the tenderness.

Because David's restraint only revealed how catastrophic his love would become without it.

His mouth moved lower against her throat.

Kissing.

Breathing.

Almost feeding.

Ember's knees weakened hard enough that David lifted her effortlessly against him.

The motion stole a gasp from her lips.

His eyes changed immediately.

Dark.

Ancient.

Starving.

And still heartbreakingly careful.

David carried her toward the velvet bench beneath the stained-glass windows.

Not hurried.

Reverent.

The crypt glowed around them like some ruined cathedral built entirely for hunger and prayer.

He lowered her slowly onto the velvet cushions without breaking contact.

His mouth returned instantly to her throat.

Ember's hands slid beneath his coat, over cold fabric and harder muscle beneath.

David shuddered violently.

The reaction wrecked her.

"You undo me," he whispered against her skin.

Then he fed.

Not from her wrist this time.

From her throat.

The sharp ache bloomed instantly beneath his mouth.

Intimate enough to feel devastating.

Deep enough to make her body tremble beneath him.

David's grip tightened against her waist while relief and hunger moved visibly through him together.

He moved one long-fingered hand beneath her skirt to gently stroke her inner thigh before his fingers found the core of her.

Ember gasped softly and clung harder to him as warmth flooded violently through her bloodstream in slow waves of pleasure and fear and unbearable attachment.

The feeding lasted longer this time.

Long enough for the room to blur.

Long enough for David's restraint to begin slipping visibly at the edges.

His breathing roughened.

His hand tightened upon her waist.

His fingers moved with increasing speed upon her core.

The hunger sharpened.

And still he held her like something sacred.

When she gasped out her completion, he finally pulled away, and both shivered.

A dark mark bloomed against Ember's throat beneath candlelight.

David stared at it with devastating intensity.

Mine.

The thought moved between them silently now.

No longer hidden.

David touched the mark gently with trembling fingers.

Then looked at her with naked hunger and naked love intertwined so tightly that they had become impossible to separate.

"If I claim you fully," he said quietly, "there is no returning to the life you had before me."

The crypt fell silent around them.

Rain above.

Candles below that.

And immortality waiting somewhere between his mouth and her pulse.

Ember looked at him and realized the answer had existed for weeks now.

Not despite the monster.

Because the monster was part of him.

Part of the hunger.

Part of the tenderness.

Part of the terrible, beautiful devotion she had already begun surrendering herself to.

So, she touched his face softly and whispered:

"I stopped wanting that life when I met you."

You kiss me first.

Beautiful girl.

Do you understand what surrender tastes like to something immortal?

It tastes warm.

Terrified.

Devoted.

You stand inside your family crypt surrounded by saints and dead bloodlines, and when I confess eternity has finally become frightening, you answer by putting your mouth on mine.

God.

You destroy me gently.

I tell you what permanence means because I cannot bear hiding it from you any longer.

Not simple turning.

Not simple hunger.

Binding.

The slow, catastrophic merging of instinct and devotion until the vampire no longer knows where they end and the chosen person begins.

I have seen vampires destroy entire cities over bonds like this.

I have watched immortals walk willingly into fire after losing the person anchoring them to eternity.

And now I understand them.

That is the horror.

Not hunger.

Love.

You ask if I have ever wanted permanence before.

No.

Never.

Not once in centuries of existence.

I have desired.

Obsessed.

Consumed.

But never this.

Never looked at another living creature and thought, I would rearrange eternity itself to keep you.

Then you kiss me.

And every remaining thread of restraint inside me tears loose at once.

You taste like rain and devotion and the final moments before disaster becomes irreversible.

When I feed from your throat, the world nearly disappears entirely.

The pulse beneath my mouth.

The pulse of your pleasure beneath my fingers.

Your body trembling against mine.

Your hands beneath my coat as though cold no longer frightens you.

You welcome the monster now.

That realization nearly drives me mad with hunger.

And still, even now, you do not understand the full danger.

If I claim you completely, I will never stop wanting you.

Never stop centering my existence around the shape of your heartbeat.

Forever is a long time for something hungry.

Yet when I warn you, there will be no returning to the life you had before me, you touch my face like mercy itself and answer without hesitation:

I stopped wanting that life when I met you.

Beautiful, ruinous girl.

You say it like you are surrendering to an overwhelming passion.

And God help me—

I think I would burn kingdoms to keep hearing it.

Chapter 15

The Claiming

THE LIGHT RAIN FOLLOWED them home from the cemetery.

It clung silver to David's black coat and dampened Ember's hair in dark waves against her throat while Marceaux House rose before them like something waiting.

Watching.

The fourth-floor hallway glowed softly beneath amber sconces as David unlocked his apartment door.

Neither of them spoke.

Not because there was nothing left to say.

Because language had begun to feel too small for whatever was happening between them now.

The crypt still lived beneath Ember's skin.

His mouth against her throat.

The trembling in his hands.

The terrifying softness in the way he said forever.

David stepped aside to let her enter first.

Always that restraint.

Always that choice.

Even now.

The apartment smelled of rain, candle wax, and old vinyl.

He was by the phonograph and suddenly a record turned softly somewhere near the bay windows. Low cello drifted through the rooms while the cemetery beyond the glass glowed pale beneath storm light.

Ember removed her coat slowly.

David watched.

Not politely.

Hungrily.

The feeding mark at her throat pulsed visibly beneath his gaze.

His jaw tightened immediately.

There.

That fracture in control again.

Ember had begun craving it.

The realization should have horrified her.

Instead, heat unfurled slowly through her bloodstream.

The apartment door closed on its own behind them.

The sound echoed softly through the rooms.

Private.

Final.

When Ember turned toward him, he stood utterly still near the window.

Black coat still damp.

Dark eyes nearly ruined with restraint.

Hands flexing once at his sides as though touching her immediately would cost him something enormous.

God.

She wanted him most like this.

Not pretending.

Not polished smooth into civility.

Hungry.

"You're staring again," she whispered softly.

David's gaze lowered slowly to her throat.

"I have stopped pretending not to."

The honesty moved through her like heat.

Ember crossed the room toward him deliberately.

No hesitation now.

No fear in asking whether she should leave.

That question had died somewhere beneath stained glass and rainwater.

Now only one remained:

How completely was she willing to belong to him?

David watched her approach with visible tension moving beneath his stillness.

"Ember."

Warning again.

But weaker every time.

She stopped directly before him.

Close enough to feel cold radiating gently from his skin.

Close enough to hear the slight roughness in his breathing.

Not human breathing.

Predatory breathing.

Beautiful breathing.

Ember lifted one hand slowly to his beautiful face.

David closed his eyes instantly at the contact.

The reaction alone nearly destroyed her composure.

“You tremble when I touch you now,” she whispered.

His throat moved once beneath pale skin.

“You should not sound pleased by that.”

“But I am.”

His eyes opened.

Dark.

Ancient.

Terrifyingly open.

The hunger there no longer frightened her.

It called to her.

That realization hit hard enough to steal the breath from her lungs.

David saw it happen.

Of course he did.

“You look at my hunger as if it is something holy,” he said quictly.

The words sounded wrecked.

Ember’s fingers slid slowly into his rain-damp hair.

“Because it is yours.”

Something inside him broke.

Not violently.

Beautifully.

David kissed her with a low sound pulled from somewhere deep and ancient inside him.

Not restrained now.

Not careful in the way he had been before.

Still reverent.

Still asking.

But no longer pretending he could survive distance.

Ember melted instantly against him.

His hands closed around her waist hard enough to pull her fully against his body while his mouth moved against hers with devastating hunger sharpened into devotion.

Rain struck the windows harder outside.

The apartment blurred.

Candles.

Vinyl.

Cemetery light.

Everything dissolved beneath the overwhelming reality of David finally kissing her without restraint between them.

Ember's fingers tightened in his hair.

David shuddered sharply against her mouth.

God.

That reaction.

She kissed him deeper, deliberately.

Testing.

Choosing.

Inviting.

David's control slipped visibly.

His hands moved upward under her sweater slowly.

Cold palms against warm skin.

The sensation shattered through her.

Ember gasped softly into his mouth.

David pulled back immediately.

Eyes darkened, nearly black now.

"Tell me to stop."

The words came rough.

Painful.

Ember stared at him.

His breathing uneven.

Hands trembling slightly against her waist.

Hunger visible everywhere now beneath elegance and old restraint.

"You still ask."

"Yes."

"Even now?"

"Especially now."

The answer devastated her.

Because he meant it.

Even starving.

Even unraveling.

He still gave her a choice.

Ember touched his face gently.

Then whispered:

"Stop holding back."

David froze.

The room went perfectly still.

Rain.

Vinyl.

Candles.

Everything suspended around those words.

His eyes closed hard.

One breath.

Another.

Then he kissed her again with enough force to send them both backward toward the bedroom.

Ember laughed softly against his mouth as David guided her through the dark apartment with hands suddenly far less careful.

Possessive now.

Hungry now.

And still devastatingly attentive to every sound she made.

The bedroom waited, candlelit and shadowed beyond the hallway.

Black silk sheets.

Velvet blankets.

Rain moving silver against the cemetery windows.

David pushed the bedroom door shut behind them without breaking the kiss.

The sound shot heat through her instantly.

Private again.

His mouth moved from hers down her throat slowly.

Kissing.

Breathing.

Worshipping.

Then lower.

The sweater slipped from one shoulder beneath his hands.

David stopped instantly.

Not because he wanted to.

Because seeing her skin seemed to physically hurt him.

Ember's pulse stumbled hard beneath her throat.

David stared at the exposed skin as if devotion had become hunger and prayer simultaneously.

"Beautiful girl," he whispered.

The words sounded reverent.

Not flirtation.

Reverence.

Ember stepped closer deliberately until his body trapped hers lightly against the edge of the bed.

"David."

His eyes lifted immediately.

"I'm here."

The answer entered her bloodstream like fire.

Not physically.

Emotionally.

Completely.

David kissed her again, slower this time.

Deeper.

His hands slid along her body as though memorizing rather than touching.

Every reaction mattered to him.

Every breath.

Every tremor.

The intimacy of that nearly undid her.

Clothing disappeared gradually between kisses and candlelight.

Not hurried.

Intentional.

David touched her as if he were terrified of damaging something sacred.

And Ember realized with devastating clarity: this was not seduction anymore.

This was devotion finally becoming physical.

His mouth returned repeatedly to the feeding mark on her throat.

Each kiss there roughened his breathing further.

Each pulse beneath her skin visibly strained what remained of his control.

"You smell like hunger now," he whispered against her throat.

The words should not have thrilled her as much as they did.

Ember's hands slid along his chest.

Cold skin.

Hard muscle.

The beautiful inhumanity of him.

David made another ruined sound low in his chest.

"Again," she whispered.

He looked at her immediately.

"What?"

"Stop pretending I only want the civilized parts of you."

God.

The reaction that moved through him.

Pain.

Need.

Relief.

David pressed his forehead hard against hers.

"You do not understand what you are asking."

"Then show me."

The room tightened instantly.

David's eyes darkened completely.

His restraint trembled visibly now.

"You are going to destroy me," he whispered.

But his mouth returned to her throat anyway.

This time when he fed, the hunger arrived as he plunged deep into her body.

Two hungers satisfied at once, one of blood, one of lust.

Hotter.

Longer.

Ember cried out softly beneath him as warmth flooded violently through her bloodstream.

Not pain.

Connection.

Something opening between them.

David held her tightly against him while he fed from her throat, his hips thrusting against hers with devastating tenderness and growing desperation.

The bond deepened instantly.

Ember felt it.

A strange pressure bloomed behind her ribs.

A second rhythm moving faintly beside her own heartbeat.

David.

Not thoughts exactly.

Impressions.

Need.

Relief.

Her.

Mine.

The word struck through her body like lightning.

Ember gasped sharply.

David pulled back instantly.

Eyes wide now.

Breathing rough.

"You felt that."

Not question.

Fear.

Wonder.

Ember touched his face with trembling fingers.

"Yes."

The room swayed softly around them.

The bond between them pulsed alive now beneath skin and blood and hunger.

David stared at her like the entire world had shifted beneath his feet.

Then, slowly, almost reverently, he pressed his forehead against hers once more.

And for the first time since meeting him—

Ember heard another heartbeat inside the silence.

Not human.

Ancient.

Starving.

And hopelessly, devastatingly in love with her.

YOU TELL ME TO stop holding back.

Beautiful girl.

Do you understand what those words sound like to something starving?

Mercy denied.

I ask for consent because I no longer trust myself to recognize where hunger ends once you are beneath my hands.

And still, you choose me.

Again.

Again.

Again.

Every instinct inside me has become centered around your yes.

When I touch your skin without restraint for the first time, my body reacts like disaster finally given permission to happen.

Cold hands.

Warm pulse.

Your breath breaking softly beneath my mouth.

God.

You do not merely tolerate the monster anymore.

You desire him most clearly when he stops pretending not to exist.

That realization devastates me.

Not because it frightens me.

Because it makes me want impossible things.

Forever.

Permanence.

You in my bed every night for centuries while rain touches cemetery glass outside.

You call my hunger holy.

No one has ever looked at it that way before.

Not once.

Fear.

Lust.

Obsession.

Terror.

I have inspired all of them.

But never reverence.

Never this terrible tenderness in the way you touch my face after feeding.

When I drink from your throat tonight, the bond opens wider between us.

You feel me.

The realization nearly stops what remains of my dead heart.

Not thoughts fully.

Not language.

Instinct.

Need.

Mine.

The word escapes before I can stop it.

Ancient.

Possessive.

Absolute.

And instead of recoiling...

you move closer.

Beautiful, ruinous girl.

You hear the hunger inside me and answer it with devotion.

I should fear what I am becoming around you.

Instead, for the first time in centuries...

I fear losing it.

Chapter 16

Forever Is a Hungry Thing

Ember woke to rain and another heartbeat.

For one disoriented moment, she lay motionless, eyes closed, beneath black silk sheets, listening to the impossible rhythm moving quietly beside her own.

Slow.

Ancient.

Steady enough to sound almost unreal.

David.

The realization spread through her body instantly.

Not thought alone.

Awareness.

The bond between them pulsed softly beneath her skin now, like something living had settled inside her bloodstream during the night.

Warmth moved low through her chest.

Need followed immediately after.

Not fear.

Not panic.

Necessity.

Ember opened her eyes slowly.

Gray dawn filtered through rain-streaked cemetery windows, turning the bedroom silver-blue beneath lingering candlelight. David lay beside her under the dark sheets, one arm curved possessively around her waist even in sleep.

Or whatever passed for sleep in creatures like him.

His face looked younger like this.

Not less dangerous.

Less guarded.

Dark hair spilled across the pillow while one pale hand rested against her stomach as though instinct itself refused distance now.

Ember stared at him quietly.

The feeding marks along her throat throbbed faintly beneath the sheets.

His.

The thought arrived naturally.

Not frightening anymore.

God.

She should have been horrified by how right it felt.

Instead, she shifted closer instinctively.

David's eyes opened immediately.

Not startled.

Aware.

Always aware.

The moment his gaze found her, relief moved visibly through him.

Tiny.

Quick.

Gone almost instantly beneath restraint.

But Ember saw it.

Interesting.

"You're here," he murmured softly.

The words struck somewhere deep inside her chest.

Not because they were romantic.

Because they sounded uncertain.

As though some ancient part of him still expected to wake alone.

Ember touched his face gently.

"Where else would I be?"

His eyes darkened instantly.

The hunger remained there.

Always.

But quieter now.

Not satisfied.

Anchored.

David turned his face slowly into her palm before he could stop himself, and touched her palm gently with his soft lips.

The intimacy of that nearly undid her.

"You slept," he said quietly.

"So did you."

"Not exactly."

A faint smile touched Ember's mouth.

"You keep saying cryptic things like that and expecting me not to ask questions."

"I expect you to ask them." His thumb brushed slowly against her waist beneath the sheets. "I simply decide which answers are survivable."

The bond pulsed softly again between them.

Ember felt it now.

His attention.

His relief.

The low, restless edge of hunger beneath his composure.

Not thoughts.

Presence.

And the terrifying thing?

Her body relaxed around it instinctively.

David noticed immediately.

Of course he did.

"You feel calmer near me now," he said quietly.

It was not triumph.

It sounded almost guilty.

Ember looked at the dark marks along her throat, reflected faintly in the rain-lit mirror on the wall across from the bed.

"Yes."

The admission settled heavily between them.

Because it was true.

She felt safer in the arms of an ancient predator than she ever had in New York.

New York.

The thought arrived strangely flat now.

Colorless.

The cramped apartment.

The condemned building.

The endless noise.

The loneliness sharp enough to ache inside crowded rooms.

It all felt impossibly distant, suddenly.

Like remembering someone else's life.

David watched her expression carefully.

"What are you thinking?"

"That I barely remember what my old life felt like anymore."

The words escaped softly.

Honest.

David went still beside her.

Not cold stillness.

Fear.

Ember felt it through the bond instantly.

Sharp.

Immediate.

"You regret that." He stated.

"No."

The answer came too quickly.

David's eyes closed briefly.

Relief again.

God.

She was recognizing how often relief moved through him now whenever she stayed.

Whenever she chose him again.

It devastated her quietly every time.

His hand slid upward slowly beneath the sheets until cold fingertips rested lightly over the marks on her throat.

Possessive.

Protective.

Sacred.

Mine.

The feeling echoed faintly across the bond.

Ember inhaled softly.

David's eyes lifted to hers instantly.

"Did you hear that?" she whispered.

A silence entered him.

Then, "Yes."

The word sounded wrecked.

The bond deepened in the quiet afterward.

Not violently.

Inevitably.

David moved closer slowly until his forehead rested against hers once more.

The gesture had become instinct between them now.

“You are changing,” he said quietly.

“Because of the bond?”

“Yes.”

Fear should have arrived harder than it did.

Instead, she felt curiosity.

Warmth.

A terrible aching desire to move even closer.

“How?”

David hesitated.

That alone frightened her more than immediate honesty would have.

“You hear me sometimes now,” he said carefully. “Not language. Instinct. Emotion.” His fingers tightened faintly against her throat. “And your body is beginning to recognize me as necessary.”

Necessary.

That word again.

It moved through her with dangerous warmth.

“You say that like it’s terrifying.”

“It is.”

Ember searched his face carefully.

“Because of what it’s doing to me?”

“No.”

The answer came instantly.

“Then why?”

David’s expression changed.

The immortal mask finally cracked completely there.

No elegance now.

No careful distance.

Only devastating truth.

“Because if I lose you now,” he said quietly, “I will not survive it.”

The room fell still.

Rain against glass.

Candles burning low.

An ancient vampire looking at her with the kind of naked emotional ruin that could level kingdoms.

Ember's chest tightened painfully.

"You don't mean emotionally."

"No."

The word barely existed.

And suddenly she understood.

Not metaphor.

Not romance exaggerated into poetry.

Literal.

The bond had reached so deeply into him that separation itself had become lethal.

God.

David looked away first.

As though ashamed, she now knew the scale of what he had allowed himself to become around her.

"I should never have let this happen."

Ember touched his face immediately.

His eyes closed with visible relief at the contact.

"But you did."

"Yes."

"And if you could undo it?"

Silence.

Long enough for the sound of rain to fill the room completely.

Then David looked at her again.

"No, I wouldn't."

The honesty shattered her.

Ember kissed him softly.

Not hunger now.

Not desperation.

Love.

The realization arrived quiet and absolute between heartbeats.

She loved him.

The monster.

The hunger.

The terrifying devotion.

All of him.

David's hands tightened instantly against her body as though the bond itself had heard the realization.

Perhaps it had.

A knock sounded suddenly through the apartment.

David froze.

Annoyance moved sharply through the bond.

Interesting.

Another knock followed.

More impatient this time.

"David," Adrien's voice called faintly through the apartment. "You've become socially alarming."

Ember laughed softly before she could stop herself.

David looked deeply unamused.

"That reaction encourages him."

"I think he'd continue regardless."

"Yes."

Another voice followed this time.

Lucien.

More serious.

"We need to speak with you."

David's jaw tightened visibly.

The possessive arm around Ember did not loosen.

Interesting again.

"You don't want me out there," she said quietly.

"No."

"Why?"

His eyes darkened.

"Because they will smell the bond immediately."

Heat rose beneath her skin.

Not embarrassment.

Something warmer.

More dangerous.

Mine.

The feeling pulsed faintly through the connection again.

David closed his eyes briefly as if he heard it too.

"God help me," he whispered.

The words sounded almost overwhelmed.

Ember touched the feeding mark on her throat lightly.

"It's already irreversible, isn't it?"

A terrible silence entered him.

Then...

"Almost."

The word landed heavily between them.

Another knock.

Adrien again.

"Lucien is trying to behave responsibly, and frankly, it's upsetting everyone."

David exhaled slowly through his nose.

Then looked back at Ember with visible reluctance.

"I need to speak to them."

"Then go."

His hand tightened immediately around her waist.

"No."

The answer came instinctively.

Possessively.

Ember stared at him.

David seemed to realize what he had said only afterward.

A shadow crossed his expression.

"This is what I mean," he said quietly. "The bond changes instinct before thought."

Ember's pulse fluttered hard enough that his gaze dropped automatically toward her throat.

God.

Everything between them had become instinct now.

David touched her face gently.

Then even more carefully.

"You still have a choice."

The words entered the room with enormous weight.

Not manipulation.

Not coercion.

Choice.

Always a choice.

"If you want your old life back," he whispered, "I will let you go before the bond finishes becoming permanent."

New York flashed briefly through Ember's mind again.

Subways.

Concrete.

Loneliness.

Colorless mornings.

Then David beside rain-lit windows.

Vinyl at midnight.

Cold hands trembling against her skin.

A heartbeat ancient enough to outlive empires, softening whenever she stayed.

Real.

He felt real.

Everything before him felt pale by comparison now.

Ember looked at the vampire who loved her enough to offer freedom while visibly breaking apart at the thought of losing her.

Then she reached slowly for his hand and intertwined their fingers.

Not answer yet.

Promise.

David stared at their joined hands as if they terrified him more than fire ever could.

And through the bond between them, Ember felt the truth moving violently beneath all his restraint:

Hope.

You intertwine your fingers with mine instead of answering immediately.

Beautiful girl.

Do you understand what hope feels like to something ancient?

Violent.

Jarring.

I offer you freedom because I love you enough to fear what staying beside me will eventually cost.

And still...

You hold my hand tighter.

The bond pulses wildly between us after that.

Not hunger now.

Not appetite.

Hope.

God.

I had forgotten how dangerous hope could become.

You lie beside me beneath rain-light and black silk with feeding marks blooming dark along your throat, and somehow you still look at me as though I am something capable of gentleness.

You should not.

You know what I am now.

What I hunger for.

What I become when restraint fractures beneath the sound of your pulse.

And still your body relaxes when I touch you.

That devastates me quietly every time.

You say New York feels unreal now.

Colorless.

I hear the truth beneath the words immediately.

You are already leaving your old life behind in ways neither of us can undo.

I should be your protector, not your downfall.

Part of me should want to stop this.

Part of me should carry you out of Marceaux House before the bond roots itself so deeply into your soul that separation becomes impossible.

Instead, I listen to your heartbeat slow beside mine and feel relief move through my body like a prayer finally answered.

Monster.

The word should shame me more than it does.

Because when I tell you I will not survive losing you, you do not recoil.

You touch my face.

Merciful girl.

No one has ever answered my hunger with mercy before.

Adrien knocks at the door.

Lucien waits in the hall.

They smell eternity beginning between us already.

And the worst part?

They are right to worry.

Because when I tell you that you still have a choice, I realize something catastrophic beneath the fear and devotion and impossible hope inside me...

If you leave now...

I will let you go.

But if you stay...

I will love you with all the terrible permanence of something that has already survived death once before.

Chapter 17

Eternal Bride

The storm arrived just after midnight.

Not ordinary rain.

A cathedral storm.

Thunder rolled over New Orleans in long, mournful waves while lightning silvered the cemetery into something ancient and unreal beyond the windows of Marceaux House.

Candles burned throughout David's apartment.

Dozens of them.

Gold flames flickered against black walls and velvet shadows while vinyl turned softly near the bay windows like the pulse of something waiting.

Ember stood at the cemetery window, wearing one of David's black shirts.

Nothing beneath it.

The fabric hung loose against her thighs while rain painted silver trails down the windows beyond her reflection.

The bond pulsed steadily beneath her skin now.

David.

Need.

Hunger.

Love.

All of it intertwined so completely that she no longer knew where one ended and the other began.

And terrifyingly—

She did not want separation anymore.

Behind her, David stood motionless near the bedroom doorway.

Watching.

Not politely.

Never politely now.

He stood shirtless, exposing pale skin marked faintly by her mouth from earlier nights. His hair fell loose around his face while storm light flashed silver across the sharp lines of his expression.

Ancient vampire.

Beautiful monster.

Her David.

The realization moved through her with devastating certainty.

Mine.

The word echoed faintly back through the bond.

David closed his eyes briefly.

God.

Ember felt the reaction move through him like pain and worship tangled together.

"You hear it constantly now," he said quietly.

She turned slowly towards him.

"Yes."

His gaze lowered instantly to the marks along her throat.

Hunger sharpened visibly across his face.

But beneath it, fear.

Not fear of himself anymore.

Fear of losing her.

Ember crossed the room toward him deliberately.

Every step felt ceremonial somehow.

Like the apartment had already become altar and grave and sanctuary all at once.

David watched her approach with visible strain beneath his stillness.

"You should still understand what this means," he murmured softly.

"I do."

"No," he said. "You understand love. You understand desire." His jaw tightened faintly. "This is something older."

Lightning flashed hard beyond the cemetery windows.

The apartment glowed white for one brief, violent second.

David's eyes darkened completely.

"If you choose this fully," he said quietly, "you will belong to me in ways neither of us can undo."

The words should have sounded monstrous.

Instead, they sounded terrified.

Ember stopped directly before him.

Close enough to feel cold drifting from his skin.

Close enough to hear the ancient heartbeat beneath the silence.

"You say that like it's a curse."

His hand lifted slowly toward her throat.

Reverent again.

Always reverent when he touched her now.

"It could become one."

"But you would never let it."

The certainty in her voice visibly shattered something inside him.

David's fingers trembled faintly against her skin.

God.

Even now.

Even here.

He still feared hurting her more than losing himself.

Ember touched his face gently.

"You gave me a choice."

"Yes."

"I'm making it."

The room went perfectly still.

Rain hammered the windows.

Candles flickered low.

The bond between them tightened sharply beneath skin and blood and hunger.

David stared at her with devastating openness.

Not predator now.

Not an immortal creature wrapped in elegance and restraint.

Only a man standing at the edge of eternity, waiting to see if she would walk into it willingly.

Ember kissed him first.

Softly.

Then deeper when his hands closed around her waist with immediate, desperate reverence.

The storm outside intensified.

Thunder rolled through the cemetery while David kissed her like a whispered prayer turning physical beneath candlelight.

No restraint remained now.

Not because he lost control.

Because she had asked him not to hold back.

The distinction mattered.

His mouth moved from hers down the line of her throat slowly, kissing every feeding mark already blooming there as though memorizing devotion directly into her skin.

Ember's fingers tangled hard in his hair.

David shuddered violently.

The reaction moved through the bond instantly.

Need.

Love.

Hunger.

Fear.

Mine.

The word echoed stronger now.

Openly.

Ember gasped softly.

David froze.

Then slowly lifted his eyes to hers.

Dark.

Ancient.

Ruined with love.

"Mine," he said aloud.

No restraint this time.

No hesitation.

The word entered her body like blood and lightning and vow all at once.

Not ownership alone.

Attention.

Claim.

Forever.

And Ember realized with devastating clarity that she had been waiting to hear him say it openly since the night she first crossed his threshold.

She touched his face carefully.

Then whispered, "Yes."

The answer nearly destroyed him.

The bond surged violently between them.

Ember felt it instantly.

His hunger opening fully.

His devotion flooding toward her.

Centuries of loneliness collapsing inward around one impossible living heartbeat.

David kissed her again with enough force to drive her backward toward the bedroom.

Candles flickered wildly in their wake.

The room beyond glowed gold and crimson beneath storm light spilling through stained-glass cemetery windows.

The black silk sheets waited undone beneath them like dark water.

David lifted her effortlessly into his arms.

Ember wrapped herself around him instinctively.

No fear now.

No hesitation.

Only surrender chosen fully and consciously.

His mouth returned repeatedly to her throat while he laid her carefully against the bed.

Kissing.

Breathing.

Worshipping.

The bond pulsed harder every time his mouth touched her skin.

Ember felt him inside her constantly now.

The ache of his hunger.

The terrible tenderness beneath it.

The overwhelming relief whenever she stayed close

David stared down at her as if something sacred had finally chosen to love him back.

"You are certain," he whispered.

The question sounded wrecked.

Not because he doubted her.

Because he desperately wanted to believe her.

Ember reached for him immediately.

"Yes."

The answer moved visibly through him.

Relief so profound it almost resembled grief.

Then the hunger rose again.

Beautiful.

Terrifying.

Ancient.

David removed the black shirt from her body slowly.

Not hurried.

Ceremonial.

His eyes followed every inch of revealed skin with devastating intensity while storm light and candle fire painted gold across her naked body.

Ember should have felt exposed.

Instead, she felt chosen.

Desired completely.

David's hands moved over her as if devotion had finally become unbearable to contain physically.

Every touch reverent.

Every kiss ruinously intimate.

He kissed down her throat again.

Then lower.

Ember's breathing broke softly beneath him as the bond sharpened every sensation until touch itself became overwhelming.

David felt everything, too.

She knew because it flooded back through their connection.

Her pulse affecting him.

Her sounds undoing him.

Her body becoming instinctively necessary to his own

The intimacy of that nearly shattered her.

"David," she whispered.

His eyes lifted instantly.

Always answering.

"I want all of you."

The confession wrecked him visibly.

Not lust alone.

Emotion.

Ancient starving emotion.

"You already have me," he said softly.

"No," Ember touched his face carefully. "All of you."

The hunger inside him surged violently.

Then, slowly … carefully …

David bared his fangs fully for the first time.

No shadows hiding them now.

No restraint disguising the monster.

Beautiful.

God.

Ember's entire body reacted instantly with heat and trembling want.

David saw it.

The devastation moving across his face nearly broke her heart.

"You desire this," he whispered.

Not arrogance.

Wonder.

Ember reached for him and guided his mouth back toward her throat willingly.

"Yes. I desire you. I love all of you."

The bond flared almost painfully bright between them.

David made a ruined sound low in his chest before feeding from her throat deeply.

Not violent.

Ceremonial.

The ache bloomed instantly beneath his mouth while warmth flooded through Ember's bloodstream hard enough to arch her body beneath him.

David held her tightly against him as hunger and devotion and ancient grief poured through the bond together.

Ember felt everything.

His loneliness.

His terror.

His unbearable love.

Mine.

The word thundered through her again.

And this time she answered through the bond itself.

Yours.

David broke apart.

The reaction slammed through him so violently that the room trembled.

Candles extinguished one by one around the bedroom.

Darkness rushed inward.

Only storm light remained now.

Silver across black silk.

Rain across cemetery glass.

An ancient vampire shaking in the arms of the woman who had chosen him forever.

David pulled back from her throat, breathing unevenly.

Blood darkened his mouth beautifully.

Ember reached up instinctively and touched it with trembling fingers.

Then brought them slowly to her own lips.

David stared at her like worship had become agony.

"Ember."

Warning.

Prayer.

Love.

She kissed him before he could stop her.

And when their mouths met again, the bond opened fully.

Not turning.

Not death.

Something stranger.

More intimate.

Their heartbeats synchronized briefly beneath the storm.

One living.

One ancient.

Then slower.

Closer.

Together.

The room blurred violently around Ember as sensation flooded every nerve beneath her skin.

David.

Rain.

Candles.

Blood.

Love.

Forever.

She felt centuries brush against her consciousness like dark wings passing through cathedral shadows.

Not memories fully.

Him.

Ancient hunger finally finding peace.

David held her against him while the storm raged around Marceaux House, and dawn waited helplessly somewhere beyond the rain-heavy sky.

And for the first time in centuries...

The monster was no longer lonely.

YOU CHOOSE ME CONSCIOUSLY.

Beautiful girl.

That is the thing that undoes me completely.

Not your blood.

Not your body.

Not even your love.

Choice.

You stand before something ancient and starving and terrible, and when I warn you what forever means, you answer by stepping closer.

No one has ever done that before.

Not once.

I tell you that you will belong to me.

The words should sound monstrous.

Possessive.

Wrong.

Instead, you look at me like vows are finally being spoken in a language your soul recognizes.

Then you say, yes.

God.

The bond tears fully open inside me.

Mine.

I say the word aloud because restraint has finally become impossible around the shape of my devotion to you.

And you answer willingly.

Yours.

Beautiful, ruinous girl.

Do you understand what you have done to something immortal?

You have made eternity gentle.

When I feed from your throat tonight, it no longer feels like appetite.

It feels sacred.

Your heartbeat changes beneath my mouth.

Your body opens willingly against mine.

The bond floods with love so overwhelming it nearly brings me to my knees beside you.

I feel your fear vanish completely.

I feel your surrender become trust instead of helplessness.

I feel you choosing forever while rain batters the windows around us like mourning and blessing intertwined.

You touch the blood on my mouth without revulsion.

No one has ever done that before, either.

Not fear.

Not horror.

Reverence.

You kiss me with my own hunger still between us, and suddenly the centuries inside me stop feeling empty.

You call me back from loneliness so completely it hurts.

The monster finally becomes peaceful in your arms.

And for the first time since death remade me...

Forever no longer feels like a punishment.

Epilogue

Marceaux House

During the seasons, the rain returned often to Marceaux House.

Some nights it arrived soft as breath against the cemetery windows.

Other nights it came cathedral-heavy, drowning the old graves in silver while thunder rolled over New Orleans like distant mourning bells.

The building remained unchanged through the years.

Candles still flickered behind velvet curtains on the fourth floor.

Vinyl still drifted softly through the halls after midnight.

White roses still appeared mysteriously beside the cemetery gates every Sunday morning.

And occasionally, new tenants whispered.

Mostly about the apartment across the hall.

The beautiful couple who never seemed to age.

The woman with dark auburn hair who stood at the bay window during storms with candlelight against her skin.

The impossibly elegant man always dressed in black beside her.

Some tenants swore they never slept.

Others claimed the man moved through the building without making a sound.

That his eyes reflected strangely in mirrors.

That the woman's throat sometimes bore faint marks like shadows of old devotion beneath lace collars and velvet ribbons.

Most dismissed the stories quickly.

New Orleans encouraged beautiful hauntings.

Marceaux House simply had two more.

On storm-heavy evenings, Ember still stood beside the cemetery windows, watching rain gather silver along the crypts below.

Decades had passed.

The cemetery remained unchanged.

Marble angels weathered slowly beneath moss and stormwater while generations of flowers appeared and disappeared across graves forgotten by everyone except the dead.

But Ember remained.

Beautiful.

Still.

Unchanged beneath candlelight.

The bond pulsed softly beneath her skin now, as naturally as breath once had.

Behind her, vinyl turned quietly through the apartment.

A cello.

Low piano.

David's favorite records.

Ember smiled faintly before he even entered the room.

The bond always warned her now.

No.

Not warned.

Welcomed.

Cold hands settled instinctively at her waist from behind while David lowered his mouth softly to the marks still visible at her throat after all these years.

Reverent.

Possessive.

Home.

"You're thinking too loudly again," he murmured against her skin.

Ember leaned back into him immediately.

"You still eavesdrop."

"Yes."

The answer warmed through her like old velvet and candlelight.

David's reflection appeared beside hers in the dark cemetery glass.

Ancient vampire.

Beautiful monster.

Still looking at her as if eternity had surprised him by becoming merciful.

Ember turned slowly within his arms.

"You know," she whispered softly, "the tenants downstairs think we're ghosts."

A faint smile touched David's mouth.

"They are not entirely wrong."

Then he chuckled, "I wonder what they make of Adrien below them?"

She smiled, "They find Adrien ... strange. And somewhat terrifying in a theatrical manner."

Rain slid slowly down the windows behind them.

The apartment glowed gold beneath candlelight while the cemetery stretched silent and eternal below Marceaux House.

Unchanged.

Like them.

David touched her face gently.

Still reverent after all this time.

Still devastating.

"Any regrets?" he asked quietly.

The question held no fear anymore.

Only wonder.

Ember looked toward the rain-dark cemetery where white roses rested against the Grant crypt below.

Then back at the immortal creature who had once stood trembling in candlelight because he feared loving her would destroy them both.

Mine.

The word moved softly through the bond.

Warm now.

Peaceful.

Ember smiled.

"Not one."

David kissed her slowly while thunder rolled over the city and vinyl crackled softly through candlelit rooms.

Beyond the windows, rain continued falling across the cemetery like time itself had finally learned how to kneel.

And inside Marceaux House...

Love remained immortal.

Thank You For Reading!

Did You Enjoy This Book?

If this story left a mark on you, tell a friend — or three.
And if you have a moment to spare, a review on Amazon or Goodreads helps keep the fire burning for indie authors like me.
Your words are our fuel. Your support is our magic.

Want to see more by V. P. Nightshade?
Visit her Author Page on Amazon
https://www.amazon.com/author/vpnightshade

Check out my YouTube Page – to listen to free stories, ASMR scripts, my music, and my poetry. Subscribe and don't forget to like and share your favorites!
https://www.youtube.com/@v.p.nightshade

Author Biography

V. P. Nightshade

V. P. Nightshade writes the kind of romance your mother warned you about—dark, delicious, and devastatingly emotional.

Author of supernatural sagas and steamy fantasy tales, she conjures vivid worlds of passion, peril, and power. From vampire courts and cursed kingdoms to alien warlords and ancient gods — where monsters love too deeply, heroes bleed beautifully, and forever comes with a price — her stories twist the knife between heat and heartbreak ... and make you beg for more.

Every page pulses with rich, sensual prose and sharp emotional tension. Her heroines are haunted and hungry for freedom. Her heroes are broken, brutal, and breathtaking. And her plots? Twisted vines of fate, prophecy, and sacrifice — where nothing is safe, not even love.

She writes from the shadows. And she writes for readers who aren't afraid to follow her there.

If you like your romance haunting, your monsters tender, and your heroes barely clinging to their sanity ... welcome to the Nightshade novels.

You've been expected.

Publishing costs are always increasing! Please don't wait; buy her novels now before the price changes!

Visit her Amazon Author page at:
https://www.amazon.com/author/vpnightshade

www.ingramcontent.com/pod-product-compliance
Lightning Source LLC
LaVergne TN
LVHW010655110826
845149LV00014B/3100